Almond Eyes, Baby Face

Pilleater

Choam Charity Publishing #001
Philadelphia, PA USA
www.asianaryanism.com

ISBN-10: 0-9989203-0-4
ISBN-13: 978-0-9989203-0-6

Second Edition,
Third Printing, 2017

Printed in the USA.

Front cartoon design by Piemboons.
http://piemboons.tumblr.com

Dedicated to

M.

...I still love you.

"Guilt licks hungrily at the transparent purpose of an unclean heart."

-Jonathan Bowden.

...My girlfriend seriously looks like Hiromi Ogashira. Ever see that pretentious Western adaptation of Shin Godzilla? It was packed that night. Every seat with a Japanophile on it. And none of them speak Japanese, and they would all equally hate Desiigner, playing half-time opening night for the 76ers. Everyone booed at him. Because he's black and basketball is a white man's "watching" sport at times. Not to digress, but I am so grateful to have someone like Zoe.

Ogashira is fictional. She was played by the same actress that did the live action for Cutie Honey. Yet, this character she performs feels all too real. Zoe is not Japanese and she is Chinese. I know those two cultures and they are not alike. I don't want to assume Chinese is Japanese and vice versa... like most Japanophiles do...

I remember watching that movie. She looks so... evil. Flat cheeks. Ugly hair. Punched in forehead. An autistic nerd. She looks like she's got an Adam's apple. An ugly first grader in a woman's body. She feels as though no one would want to be around her. But then again, she was tantalizing for those reasons alone.

Is she a sadist? I had a previous Chinese girlfriend who was a sadist. I thought it was love. She bit my dick, hard. Left a scab on it. She was fat, brown, and ugly. She watched a lot of anime and was into online sex role playing. I could not trust her. She was a prude, but ironically, wished to express herself through sex. She told me she was going to blackmail me by throwing me in the closet and calling the cops on me if I ever touched her without her consent.

Blackmailing me as a rapist. Seriously, that girl had problems.

But unlike Ogashira… cute. Adorable. I feel… I see her pain. I see it in Zoe's face. The Chinese have pushed-in faces, like a square head and cuts for eyes. Unlike the Japanese, they have these almond eyes, baby face thing to them. It's why whites dream of sleeping with Japanese, but then end up getting a whitewashed Chinese American or Chinese-in-America that speaks mediocre English. I prefer Chinese over Japanese. I just have no experience with the Japanese… Even though I took two years of Japanese classes, I met Zoe in one, and other Asian classes where I had Japanese friends. But did I ever have sex or date a Japanese? Not really. There was only a case with two Japanese I dated, Ami and Skylar. I believe both had White dads and Japanese moms. Is that really authentic? Nope. I am sick of those college-educated white males that date Chinese girls and imply they are Japanese, or assume life is like an anime and project their perverted fantasies on to these girls…

Well, I am just sympathetic to Zoe. I think she understands me.

…I should log into Facebook and check whether there is class tomorrow morning. It was raining today and I had the morning classes. This is my last semester. Zoe is unfortunately a junior. I cannot walk and graduate with her. I would be back home for a year doing nothing while she is alone for a year at this state school (I'm a little attached to her now and I wish she could feel the same way about me).

So, I have to write my homework about "Affordable Health Care" and it's really something I could care less about. I know about Obamacare and how much it's a soft-form of socialism. And the whole point of paying for something no one wants to get. I get it. Too many people are in America. And America resorts to a system of feeding the idiot masses. …Am I one of those people? I am grateful to be happy at this moment.

I am grateful Zoe understands where I am coming from. All I have to do is to "be myself," and she will love me for who I am. A soon-to-be-husband, a hard-working college student, an intelligent person, and someone that might get a high paying job. That's all the charm you really need to woo over a Chinese girl. It doesn't matter if you're ugly or socially awkward. They are there with open-arms… Unlike those Japanese bitches that prefer the white men with the highest income and achievements… Annoying. The Japanese are seriously the Asian Jews. Don't ask why. Just be around them for five years and you will see.

…No class tomorrow morning. I can get back in bed. I have no friends on Facebook status…. I don't use Facebook. I use YTMND. I am still an Internet troll! Never told Zoe about it. Some parts of me are far too avant-garde… eccentric. I should belong to the Yale Art school. But my own social class tells me I belong in bumfuck, middle of nowhere (Paul Fussell, thank you). I don't like to talk about it.

Depeche Mode's *In Your Room (Zephyr Mix)* really cheers me up. Turning it up, then back to low volume. I feel awkward getting back in bed with her, you know, without some dry humps on her blue striped panties. …Cute blue striped panties. The kind of panties in those high school animes. Can you believe that? She's Chinese and wears that!

This song, the video, reminds me of being in an airplane, looking out the window, going through orange clouds, heading towards Miami. I was only… 8 at that time? And the song is like… so old. And playing it at a time when in, say 1998, five years after its original release. Music videos on airplanes. Those little TVs too. It gives me such a deep purpose in life. A deep fire in my stomach. I don't know how to explain it.

The video is so 90s. I love Dave Gahan. He is kind of a role-model to me. Even though I don't know him, I fantasize about his life. I would not want to go on a drug overdose or anything. Just sing to crowds for the rest of my life about the passions of other people. I guess that's why Gahan hates his life so much.

In Your Room… what a powerful song.

In your room
Where time stands still
Or moves at your will
Will you let the morning come soon?
Or will you leave me lying here?

That room. Room of what? Room of sex? Room of passion? Of love? When two freshmen tween-teenagers, decided to be boyfriend and girlfriend? When they decide to hang out at their dorms on a rainy day? And hug and cuddle like time will never end? I always think that WAS

4

supposed to be the purpose of going to college. You know, to meet your significant lover. I don't care about the other things, like sports, philosophy, teachers, or esoteric things to know. College benefited me with the Japanese language and learning how to write English correctly. I wished I would've known these things when I was a teenager.

In your room
Where souls disappear
Only you exist here
Will you lead me to your armchair?
Or leave me lying here?
Your favorite innocence
Your favorite prize
Your favorite smile
Your favorite slave

…How powerful it is. Only Zoe exists in this room. I'm daydreaming now. I feel like I'm still on the wrestling team when I was 14. I was playing for my Middle-school. And… I thought to myself. "That day is coming. That day when I'll get a *girlfriend*. That day when she will become my *wife*. All I need to do is wait until she sees me. I might even meet her in wrestling!" And the thing was, because I was so bad at wrestling, that I would just walk around on foreign campuses and listen to Placebo on my iPod. Waiting until I get called on. *Special K* is such a special song. I was so skinny and frail at the time. I still am. I did get a little bigger. Maybe my belly got larger. My legs too. I still try and lift weights. …Who cares? I'm not Jack Donovan.

In your room
Your burning eyes
Cause flames to arise

Will you let the fire die down soon?
Or will I always be here?

…Her burning eyes. Flames in my stomach. I wish I could write good poetry. Without writing rhyme words like "dog" and "bog." It's better to write it out sometimes. Poetry is too confusing.

I'm hanging on your words
Living on your breath
Feeling with your skin
Will I always be here?

Even if I was to not see Zoe ever again, which I'm afraid will happen soon, I will always be "living on her breath." I will "always be here" with her. In her memory, I hope. I hope I am her ideal white boy. The boy who she had sex with in college and the boy that burns her desire for white cock. …Is my white cock ideal for her? It's what she dreams about before she masturbates. What she desires. All her white boys who she wants must be like me. Not to sound possessive, but it's close to the truth! It's the same thought with all these white young adults and their first Asian (Chinese) girlfriends. "I must be the one!" "I must be her one and only white cock!" "This is the girl, who I put my white cock inside of!" "Her gushy vagina!" "So hot and steamy." "I never felt an experience like this before and will only feel it with her." "Forever and ever!" And I *will always be here* with her.

…I am looking at a piece of writing I did when I was 21. It was for creative writing class. I can't help but to copy and paste it. Read it, if you dare. It's getting really late, and my fingers are losing the pressure to type. I sent this piece to Rachel Haywire. Everyone now hates her in the Alt-right, but I still like her. Before the whole Ann fiasco, she was going to publish it in *Trigger Warning*.

I remember the day I was forced to commentate on "Nana's Song" in front of the whole creative writing class. I didn't know any better. I got sneers and snickers. I felt like a loser. The feminist teacher said… "and now, we are going to talk about Joe's piece. So… what is this?" I really didn't know what to say. I said something like it is "postmodern art and you have to take the advice of Francis Bacon to understand." One kid who really liked it called it the re-telling of the Life of Brian but I don't claim that was its intention either. I said I really liked… the art of Netrunner.

It went something like this…

4/5/13

Nana's Song

It was decided that this would be the last game of Mahjong for tonight. Nana and Portman version were north to south, and Gerald and Hanamichi were east to west. Nana's liquid screen glared 'LOADING' to process her current hand.

"Aeh-Aeh-Aeh-Aeh, Shohoku #1, tilt dat jon again", Gerald pointed out to Hanamichi. Portman whacked her palm on Nana's monitor as if she heard it for the thousandth time. Nana's screen went black, and five seconds later, her face reappeared.

"Ready to play mahjong?", she said in her OSX Laila preset. She was also the jukebox. She played on very low, *Mouse on Mars - Schnick Schnack Meltmade*. It gave some sort of fringe comfort to every board game night.

The last hand finally went out. "Alright, dis is mah best yet", Gerald said between him and Nana.

Both Hanamichi and Portman would've rather played Netrunner tonight. Portman had no chance of winning this one. She gazed up at the neon light, too bored to smoke again. Hanamichi passed her tiles anyway. The gibberish tune kept them alive.

"Aight stick him up Nansta!", Gerald said with the utmost confidence. Suddenly, Nana turned off *Meltmade*. Portman looked up.

Nana talked using a sequence of herself from different issues archived in memory. She had a voice file for every English vowel; spanning from an E still from Vol.1 and the classic O from Vol.2, almost looking like a sex doll.

"Hey guys, I've been practicing with my killer bannnd (a lag in speech) recently. Would you like to hear a song me and NANA (loud) did?" She would break down like this during a game. It was her way of saying she lost.

"Nansta, wuts in yo hand? Stop bein' a sour faggot and show me whatcha you got!"

"Not again", Portman said.

It was embarrassing that Nana could not even remember in her circuits that Nana Portman was the musician and she was the housemaid.

"Nana, you wanna go now? I got some soma at my cell", Hanamichi said. He had a chance with this woman than the girl who broke up, Haruko, even though he still thinks about her every week. Everyone had anxiety issues when *Meltmade* wasn't on.

The room turned dark by Nana's orders. She also controlled the room. "Okay guys, here I go". Nana's screen went black, the orange neon light was the only thing alive. Gerald stared at the screen, mouth open. Hanamichi and Portman did not feel like it. Whenever she sang, her stills would animate in motion. It was awkward and not possible for her computing. She sang in-sync with the cut-up samples:

In your heart, there's a world of sadness, I love you with all heart.

Love is like a bullet in the head - uh huh.

What you heard is never really what I said - uh huh.

Always the war in 1983 - this is the world of today.

In our mind, there is only the money and there is nothing for you.

Then hours work no flowers in the mind.

She's got the look (she's got the look!)

You said that you loved me And I thought that it was true
You said that you needed me. And baby, I believed that too.

And if I should start to cry,

and I can't begin to tell you why,

and I stumble when I begin,

it's 'cause I don't understand anything.

(You reach for me from miles away,)

You're a danger, you're a stranger.

Got to know the way to make you mine.

Come on dancer give me a chance and

Make me love until the end of time.

KISS ME KISS ME BABY so you can tell me why.

Take me take me up to the sky.

KISS ME KISS ME BABY so you can try me now.

Tell me tell me watching the moonlight.

Kiss me baby don't worry I'm your lover.

I'm in action for you, darling.

Kiss me honey don't trust me like a cover.

Still alive my love for you.

…Portman took a long sigh. Nana was not done yet. Hanamichi worried. He got up with her.

I'm not afraid of the price I pay.

I won't lie down as you walk away.

I know you must have seen him.

I'm sure you must have heard it all.

I know you used to be him.

Did anybody care at all?

My eyes gain focus the second you walk in.

Feathers of evil shaking and burning.

Daddy, oh daddy, oh daddy, you're listening.

I know that they're dirty, I know that they're faking.

So, what kind of voodoo do you do to make me feel this way?

What kind of voodoo do you do to make me feel this way?

As soon as you turn up my skin starts to burn up.

I burn up I burn up.

As soon as you turn up.

So, what kind of voodoo do you do?

What kind of voodoo do you do?

What kind of voodoo do you do to make me feel this way?

Up in flames.

Up in flames.

Up in flames.

My love will go up in flames for you.

Profoundly profane and it drives me insane.

[Noise] - What do you know - Don't blow your top now, here we go!

Ingenuity and progress never progressed out of the sun.

All experiments prove not need the established.

Greed and pain inflicted on the animal model still nothing.

No cure the ravaged instinct silent waking to a

Chemical perversion wartime underground.

Imperfect plotting grows the seeds of time.

Imperfect plotting grows the seeds of time.

Imperfect plotting grows the seeds of time.

Imperfect plotting grows the seeds of time.

 The song was over and the lights went back on slowly. Portman and Hanamichi rushed out the then sealed door. Gerald became fascinated. He could care less about the game now. He shook his head, "Yo, dat beat "like, I like.

But seriously, lay off dat one part about the black celebration, no way mang."

Gerald had a lot to say about politics. Only Nana listened to his ramblings. He was black, a midget, and a committed Zionist. Hence, he always wore that same large size Star of David t-shirt. Gerald stood on the table, on the tiles, face to face with Nana. "Yo music, know wut it's like? It's candy-coated! Bullshit!" Waving his hands spastically as he talked, "Do you wanna make music that's ill or do you want to make music that evokes the masses.

You know what George Lincoln Rockwell said? I quote, 'The masses of people will not study! They read comic books, they look to go see the TV, they like to read dime-novels, and they will not study like us Nazis do. The masses of people liked being entertained and everything you give them must be sugarcoated.' I repeat, 'sugarcoated'. "Nansta, if you want to make a bettah chune, it can't be sugarcoated! Aight? Stop makin chunes what they like and make songs that mean somethin, got dat!?" Gerald finished, "Rockwell, dats who you should respect, Rockwell, mah hero!"

It was silent for a bit. Nana computed his criticism. "You're a nice boyfriend! How's about a game of Mahjong?"

Gerald got off the table, "Bitch-ass computer, don't mean shit. Aight you shuffle this time." Gerald stayed for the second game. Nana was his best friend.

THE END.

And then this happens…

"What are you doing?" Zoe says.

"Nothing, I'll coming back in," Joe responded. She gets out of bed, knees sinking into the mattress on the floor, hands pushing Joe's back. Joe is shocked. Zoe laughs.

"What's that?"

"My homework."

"No, it's not. Looks like you're doing something else."

"Well, that's my old story I wrote in creative class. It's called 'Nana's Song.' It's kind of… experimental?"

Zoe looks at Joe's Macbook Air. She squints her eyes (her eyes are darker and small enough).

"What is this?"

"Something stupid. I don't know."

"It's not bad. It looks good."

"It's one of those stories, where I just tried to make up one. It's kind of about myself, about the music I listen to, the art I like, some movies I saw… I was trying to be like someone."

Zoe is reading it. Joe is awkwardly closing off pages of Facebook, Counter-Currents, other websites that girls would not like. Trying to act normal. Zoe's head on Joe's shoulder is already anxious enough.

"Is this a comedy?"

"Yeah, they're playing poker and then it starts to sing songs I like."

"Haha. That's funny."

"Um… yeah."

Zoe looks at the clock.

"It's 11:30. Get in bed."

"With you?" Joe smiled. "I don't want to sleep on the sofa again."

"Of course not! I like you!"

"Ok. …I am very grateful Zoe. You're such a nice person."

"Haha, Ok."

Joe got up to go change in the room. While doing that, he looked back really quick at Zoe's cute butt. Such a nice body.

That's what happened last night. I did sleep with her. I love sleeping with her. No sex or anything. This kind of sleep, where I feel everything is good in life. All my anxiety is gone. I just hope Zoe can like me forever. Zoe is such a great person. I could go on and on about her personality and how beautiful she is.

I don't care what other people say about her. She is somewhat sickly. She does takes some pills because of a condition I can't explain. But no, she is not a drug addict.

And her cute clothes she wears every day and that choker collar she's been wearing now when we go out. She looks so good. No, she's not into *that* kind of sex. She's just playing around. I wish the whole world knows that I belong with her.

After college, I want to marry her. I plan on it.

You're now chatting with a random stranger. Say hi!

You both like Sex Roleplay.

You: F

Stranger: Hi, M19.

You: Awesome!

You: How are you? :)

Stranger: I'm fine and horny:) how about you? ^^

You: Great!

You: What are you doing up at this late hour?

You: Huh?

Stranger: Well, wanted to do some roleplay after a long time, mainly because I just couldn't sleep and didn't know what else to do :D How about you?

You: Aww yeah!

You: What's your name sweetie?

Stranger: Chris, how about yours?

You: Ying, but I prefer Zoe :)

Stranger: Damn I'm repeating myself so much? :D

Stranger: Great name btw!

You: Haha thank you!

You: So, what do you do late this hour?

You: Chromecast and cuddle?

You: lol.

Stranger: I think cuddle lol.

You: What? No Netflix? haha.

You: I fucking love Spongebob. Wearing pink Spongebob pajamas now.

Stranger: Wow, that actually sounds hot.

You: Haha, I knew you would say that! :)

You: I think you would be more into my black hair.

Stranger: Aw yeah? How would you like if I just grabbed it and pulled your head to mine so I could kiss you? :=

You: Hahaha. You are the romantic?

You: :)

Stranger: Dunno about that.

You: Or you just saying that?

Stranger: Just saying.

You: Cool jazz.

You: What else would you do? ;)

Stranger: Definitely would take your clothes off :P

You: Haha! you're so eager!

You: It's so hot in here!

You: Idk if it's the city outside or if the room is too small.

Stranger: Hehe.. I just got a hard on from you :P Definitely would love to put my cockhead on your pussy and just play there a little bit..

You: Haha, yeah, I got no panties on!

You: I haven't seen it before,

You: You kiss and say stuff, but let me really see it!

You: Are white dude's cocks really that big ;)

Stranger: Depends :P I have about 7 inches btw :P

You: Get out. :p

You: Why are you after me then?

Stranger: It's already out baby.

You: Whhhaaaaattt!

You: LOL.

You: Ahhhhhh.

You: It's so pink XD

You: It's a stick! hahahaha.

Stranger: Well...that's a reaction, lol.

Stranger: Wanna touch it? :P

You: Omg lol hahaha.

You: get it anyways XD

You: Wow.

You: What are you doing? Get in bed!

You: You're just standing there.

Stranger: Mmm… as you wish baby :P

You: Hahah.

You: It's like an animal dick.

You: Aha!

You: Trying to put it on my leg?

Stranger: Ahh… you talking about my cock like this makes me sooo horny to be honest.

Stranger: Here you go :*

You: Haha.

You: It tickles when you brush it on me.

Stranger: It tickles my cockhead too lol.

You: Guys always say that about their cock.

You: Haha lol.

Stranger: Ah.

Stranger: You mean it like this XD

You: Yeah, no shit, my pussy is hard too!

You: Hahaha :)

You: Omg shhhhhhh.

Stranger: Mmmm.. lemme touch it with my fingers :P

You: My roommate is in the other room!

You: I don't want her to hear me fucking my boyfriend at this hour haha.

Stranger: Awh okay haha.

You: Shhh.

You: Haha.

You: Ok.

You: Lights out.

You: Kiss me :)

You: Under the sheets.

Stranger: Mmm :*

You: :>

You: :)

You: You like when I touch it?

You: <3

Stranger: Yea, baby... feels soo good...

Stranger: :3

You: I bet you never had a girl on your cock before! haha!

You: Cutie!

You: Kiss.

You: And your balls!

Stranger: :==

You: Haha.

You: Like when I treat them like this?

You: Haha.

Stranger: Awww God hell yeah hah.

You: Hah, balls are so strange.

You: Or like.

You: What if I slap them?

You: You will get hurt! XD

Stranger: Ohh cmon.

You: Haha :)

You: Ok.

Stranger: You can't even realise how much it hurts :D

You: Yeah.

You: I'm turning red from this excitement.

You: Ok.

Stranger: Aww sweet!

You: Turn me over.

You: Just let me face the wall.

You: To the right.

Stranger: Mmm, yeah...

You: Ok so.

You: Just pull down my pants.

You: And you know.

You: Just like…

You: Put your stick around it ;)

You: Do it soft.

Stranger: Sure baby :P

You: Can't do rough tonight!

Stranger: Anything you say :*

You: Haha.

Stranger: I mean everything hah.

You: Your hand is so sticky!

You: And warm

You: On my butt.

Stranger: Mmm... what happens if I slap it a little? :P

You: Haha.

You: Ouch.

Stranger: Mmm...

You: Omg.

You: You're strong!

Stranger: Wasn't everything I got baby :P how about this... mmm..

You: I know you love Chinese ass!

You: OH.

You: ahhhh XD

Stranger: I love this ass of yours baby :P

You: Put your arms around mine.

You: Yeah.

Stranger: Alright.

You: Haha, my long hair is touching your cock.

You: I can feel it. So strange.

Stranger: Awhh.

You: Yeah.

You: Chris.

You: Yes.

You: Keep going.

Stranger: Mmm, yes,..

You: Baby.

You: I feel it.

You: So good.

You: Yes.

You: Baby.

Stranger: I love that baby:*

You: I love you.

You: Yes.

You: :)

You: Haha.

You: I'm getting wet.

Stranger: Mmm… my cock is rock hard all the time :3

You: Yeah.

You: Haha.

You: Feels like I'm outside.

You: Feels like a monster on me.

Stranger: Can I play with your tits a little, baby?:* Come here..

Stranger: Mmm...

You: What? haha.

You: You like a flat chest?

You: Ahhhh.

You: I love you so much.

Stranger: Yeah.. the nipples...

You: You're crazy!

Stranger: Let me just suck on them a little...

Stranger: Mmm... :33

You: Ahhhh

You: Now you're being perverted.

You: Oooo.

You: Such a cute beast you are.

You: <3

You: Kiss.

Stranger: Mmm, yeah :==

You: Kiss me.

Stranger: :== mm

You: Long kiss.

You: Taste me.

You: Wrap your hand around my head.

You: :)

Stranger: Yes, baby :* lemme put my tongue into your mouth..

You: Your kisses.

Stranger: So I can play with yours...

Stranger: Mmm :*

You: Are so sloppy :p

You: Kiss.

You: I love you.

You: You're such a nice guy.

Stranger: I love you too, baby:*

You: :))

You: Cum on my leg.

Stranger: Awwww.

You: Jerk it.

You: It.

Stranger: You're this perverted? <3

You: It's so powerful!

You: Quick.

You: You're not wearing a condom!

Stranger: Mmmm.. gonna cum really soon.. ahhh…

You: You're an animal!

You: Honey.

Stranger: Here.. on your leg... ahhh!

You: OO

Stranger: I'm cumming...

You: AHHH.

You: Haha.

You: Lol.

You: Wow.

You: Hahaa.

You: It's like you're peeing.

You: With white goop.

You: Lol.

Stranger: Awhh… yeahh.

You: Omg.

You: Let me kiss it!

You: <3

Stranger: Ahhh, yes baby... I'm loving these kind of kisses. :33

You: Nice man.

You: This is mine <3

You: You're gonna look out for me.

Stranger: All yours :*

You: Take a pic of my leg.

You: Don't show it to anyone!

You: Hold on.

Stranger: Yes, baby, I promise.

You: Another pic.

You: Like me get one with your cock.

Stranger: Mmm...

Stranger: Here...

You: Cock selfie!

You: Omg, lol.

Stranger: Awhh haha.

You: Kiss.

You: Suck.

You: Awww :)

Stranger: You can't actually imagine how much I'm enjoying this... :**

You: I love your white cock <3

You: So glad I met you.

You: Foreplay me.

You: Come here.

You: Kiss me more :)

You: I love you baby.

Stranger: Mmm... :** kiss

You: Mmm.

You: I love you.

Stranger: I love you too :3 mm... my cock is all rock hard again from you... mm

You: You're so soft <3

You: Yeah.

You: Sweating.

You: :)

You: Oh, it's so hot out.

Stranger: Yeah...

You: What time is it?

Stranger: Don't even know anymore baby.

You: Haha.

You: Bend over.

Stranger: Mmm, yeah?

You: What is it?

Stranger: I don't know baby... really...

You: Yeah fuck it.

You: :)

You: Mmm.

You: Let me lay on your chest.

You: Close the window, the city is too noisy.

Stranger: Alright ... come on my chest baby :*

You: :)

You: Kiss.

You: Yeah.

Stranger: Wshh your tits... mmm

You: Hehehehehe.

You: You can cum twice?

You: ;)

Stranger: For you? of course baby :**

You: Hehe.

You: I feel so safe.

Stranger: Mmm... as you should when you are this close to me :*

You: :)

You: I love your whisper.

You: :)

Stranger: Mmm... how about whispering into your ear how much I love you ? <3

You: :)

You: Haha.

You: I feel so slow now.

You: And tired.

You: You're such a great guy.

Stranger: Ahh, thanks baby :3

You: :3 You too

You: :)

You: What's happening tomorrow?

You: My left leg is so sticky ha.

You: Sticky.

Stranger: Haha, put it here so I can make it even stickier with my cockhead with precum :==

Stranger: Ahh...

You: Haha.

You: Get it away! :)

Stranger: Mmkay baby.

You: Mom is coming over tomorrow.

You: You gotta look good!

Stranger: Ohh alright.

You: No jock shit like you like to do :P

You: Or any of that "bro" stuff.

Stranger: Ahh c'mon haha.

You: I just you to leave a good impression on her.

You: I want to be with you :)

Stranger: So do I baby.

Stranger: Alright.

Stranger: Will do.

Stranger: For you :*

You: :)

You: You're so sweet.

You: You know...

You: We are totally gonna have 4 kids! lol

Stranger: Ahh you want 4.

Stranger: Wow.

You: Haha.

You: We can do it!

Stranger: Sure thing:*

You: Two sons, two daughters?

You: Or all sons or girls?

Stranger: Dunno, I think two and two sounds the best.

Stranger: What do you think?

You: Hopefully so :)

You: Zoe, Chris Jr.... I love "Alice" great names.

Stranger: Mmm, sounds great baby!

You: Baozhai!

You: Mom's name

You: Just call her "Betty" haha.

You: :)

Stranger: Mmm, okay baby :)

You: Well, there's tomorrow!

You: Let me lay on you.

Stranger: Yup.

You: Go to sleep dear ;)

Stranger: Mmm... wanted to cum for you for the second time but okay baby ^^ whatever you want :3

You: Ahhhhhaahah.

You: Cut it out.

You: !

You: :)

You: Let me kiss it goodnight.

You: Kiss.

You: Already too soft.

Stranger: Mmm yeah.

You: I'll suck it like ramen noodles lol.

You: You're a fucking stud.

Stranger: Awwww baby.

Stranger: Cmon, you know how this turns me on.

You: Guy's dicks are so strange.

Stranger: Why do you think so baby?

You: Little red tip and everything.

You: I laugh when I see yours!

Stranger: Well the tip is the most sensitive part... ahhh cmon!

Stranger: Haha.

You: :)

You: Aha.

You: Go to sleep dear.

You: Goodnight Chris <3

Stranger: Goodnight Zoe <3

You: ;) <3

Stranger: Ntw wanna do the morning or you are leaving?

You: Wut?

Stranger: Well

Stranger: We just went to sleep in the role play right?

You: Go to bed dear haha.

You: 爱

You: Or kik me.

Stranger: I already am in the bed :D okay but I prefer Skype if you have it.

Stranger: What's your kik?

You: Umm, I gotta go babe. Whatever.

You have disconnected.

***

Why did this happen to me? All I did was transfer to this new school to get out with a BA. And then, I had to stay there for two years! Why? I spent a total of 5 years in college. Right? And starting this habit at the age of 19, quickly turning 20 on my birthday week. And getting out, when I'm 25. I still feel like I've been used. I feel old. I feel like a loser. And this private school I have gone to, whose name I will not speak, is a joke. Driving in my car, every morning, and driving back home, every day! My parents' house is my dorm and the school is… work. I really wanted to succeed.

I had too much fun as an Asian Studies major. I have been to several different colleges, and this college, the one I hate, is the one I have to graduate from. I had to choose "English and Communications," without a choice. I didn't know my own self during these early years. The classes I took for fun were the classes I would end up getting a major in. I do not want to take an extra two years to get a major in Asian Studies. I would rather be on a "Disney vacation trip."

And then there is this "college experience." The very thing I hate about college. The thing that causes me anxiety, stress, deludes me of reality. What is it anyway? Am I a loser in a game where I was never told what the rules were about? And to learn *the important* rules, I had to watch people, and watch them do stupid things. I had to read about "Game" blogs, about "Roosh the Doosh" and his rape memoirs. Are white girls that stupid? Yes, they are. I can't be myself in the institution which is called "college." It is a joke. The masses never deserved to go to college in the first place. This would have mattered if I'd got into Penn, Yale, or Harvard. And they would've said to me, "you should've at least tried to get in!" And I would have said back a simple "no." Why does it matter? Being a crazy, eccentric, bourgeois person? What is the meaning of life anyway? My parents told me to go to school because they never had the chance to go. I am grateful to them for giving me the chance to go.

But in this age, where I sacrifice my good youth, in favor of becoming a disturbed intellect, a race-realist, a prudish person, I must ask, "why did I not get the things I deserve?" I did not get promiscuous sex in school, I did get good friends, I did not get access to exotic places I can travel. Not even the knowledge to go work for someone or make a connection. Rather, I watched people do these things while I suffered. By existing, I did not get these things. It's not enough to be myself. The pre-socratic people will abuse the socratic people and make an abstract world full of lies… and then they say college is the best years of your life! Really? Is this the best years of my life? What is it then? Am I still too young to understand what is real and what is meaningful? Did I have abusive parents and lose my confidence becoming independent and atomized? (Is that even a good thing or is that part of the problem?) Do I have to make enough to do these perverted things? And the people with the most money get to do better things than me? Do I suffer under these things and should I become a Marxist? I don't know anymore.

The only thing I learned in college… is that the good thing in life is getting laid. And the worse part of life's ugliness, and death, is around every corner. Give it 60 years. Life is an anxious countdown before that day comes. And so, America, The West, throws itself on saving "the innocent" when really they mean giving maximum benefits to those that want to "live fast, die young." And I was told that "growing-up" and becoming an "adult" was a good thing. Brian Aldiss once said that "adults are merely the corpse of dead children." Nothing could be truer than that. And for every 20-year-old idiot that says, "I am an adult now." No, you're not. You are a privileged idiot looking for excuse to commit acts of murder. I swear this is real. Maybe when I become 30, I will realize my potential as a person. I hate being "young." I love beauty, health and muscles, but I hate this market concept of "youth." Doing stupid things. Being so pretentious. Every day is another reason why I wish I was Chinese instead. East Asian culture seems so better for us. We don't know.

And the reason why Asian girls saved my life.

But it's not about them right now, it's about this one girl I have to see every day of my life until this December. Her name is Sophie.

And her boyfriend is Justin. Sophie, the only Chinese on this Goddamn, forsaken, stuff-white-people-like campus. And she goes out with Justin. The only white male that approached her. This Sophie started to appear in my English classes last year. I didn't care for her! But now, like Chinese Water Torture itself, I cannot stand it! To see Justin kiss Sophie every day before class. Before it begins and after class… What is the meaning of my existence anymore? I had to tell my crazy Chinese girlfriend that I liked Sophie more. That bitch got pissed off at me, and now we don't date. You see, I am mad now. That's how I now know what it feels to be a loser.

I see Justin as this orbital beta-male cuck within him. He never once talked to me. I tried to talk to him. I pointed out his cool Sailor moon t-shirt, and he does not care. Oh well. He's way too shy. And he wears his stupid Mega Man t-shirt in my social justice class. (what a joke SJW class is! Already, you can see why I am in pain so much!) And then the way he talks. Whiney and still young. And he hardly talks in this class at all! And that time when I went to the bathroom, Justin refused to piss next to me, and he went in the bathroom stall instead like a girl! Too shy to flip his dick out right next to me! Not a man.

And then Sophie, and stickers on her laptop. It makes me mad. So, angry, I can't even look upon those stickers. I can't even see the meaning behind every sticker. I am not allowed to be a part of her club... TO STICK MY DICK IN HER VAGINA! MY WHITE COCK! What does she have on her laptop? A sticker of... Pikachu? Of... Mega Man? For Christ sake, does she only like Mega Man because Justin likes it too? Is she a tool? She's from Maryland, I know that much. And she herself, does not want to talk in class. Just like her little, cute, boyfriend... *Justin*. Justin! And my crazy Chinese girlfriend tells me to go and fight him and protect Sophie? ...What is there to like in me? That day, earlier this year, I pretended to be serious, and she asked something. I forget. "Yeah sure," I said. And today I saw her walk down the stairs I go to walk up. Too afraid to say hi. Too afraid to talk to her. I don't respect Justin. I am jealous. This is the "White Female Asian Female" couple at... *this* college (Erik Erikson). And I cannot *be* the one who deserves? The one who speaks Japanese? The one that is disciplined and passionate??

My anger goes all the way back to high school. You see, I was the eccentric artist that liked Juxtapoz magazine, the only one that like Electronic music, and the only one that was a musician and went to concerts at the age of 15!? The best artist of school... None other than *Ryan* and *Lauren*.

(You see where this is going? Again, White Male Asian Female. Still, I'm the one left out).

My hatred is geared towards white women... but my hatred is growing for these white males. These white males that are orbital and beta cucks. Ask any of them "Wow, your girlfriend is hot, I wish I had a Asian girlfriend," And then you get it from this sad Ryan person... "No! It's not about that at all! It's about love! I love her! I don't see her for what she is."

What a pathetic cuck. I don't hate myself because I am a white male. In fact, my last Chinese girlfriend broke up with me because she thought The Turner Diaries were too close to my political beliefs. And she left me. Stupid bitch.

And that Justin. I saw him have on his ring finger a wedding ring. IS THAT MOTHERFUCKER GOING TO MARRY SOPHIE? What a geek! I am mad and upset now.

And that's when it's time to go to next class... I will have to write later...

An Email exchange between two young blokes. Censored for private reasons.

Gaski!

I am a huge fan of your works and your translation with [CENSORED]!

I recently recorded two interviews on [CENSORED].

My name is Steve and I actually created an account on [CENSORED] to thank you so much for your work! (You did reply, not sure if you can recall the name...X).

I am asking you, **would you like to be interviewed on [CENSORED] about your career and some thoughts about Yaoi and [CENSORED]?**

This interview would be conducted on Skype and recorded audio. It would feature [CENSORED] ...it's a variety show that features many different voices from eccentric people and artists, with the intention of an "alt-left." Not exactly alt-right!

[CENSORED] had an interest in you, since I did talk about [CENSORED] and its influence on me. It is such a great show and your devotion to [CENSORED] is what made it possible!

I hope we can get in contact!

-Steve P.

—

Hello. Thank you, and I really appreciate the offer and wish the best for you.

I apologize, but I'm afraid I'll have to decline. While I am flattered, I grew up with a pretty bad speech impediment and have always been averse to doing things like audio commentary even to this day. It's just something I never got comfortable with because I never liked hearing myself, even after speech therapy and such.

If you need anything else, please feel free to ask. I'm sorry I can't do it. Good luck with your show.

~Gaski

—

I understand.

I just want to say I am a huge fan of yours and you are responsible for getting [CENSORED] to an English audience.

Although I would consider a written interview, unfortunately, I have no questions to think of at the moment and cannot find a publication. A vocal interview would be more effective to a listening audience.

You have such an interesting personality. Whatever you do, you work is great.

-Steve P.

—

Thank you. It's a little strange to be told I have a fan, because it's hard to even imagine. If you do think of any questions, feel free to ask. I'm not sure how entertaining or informative I can be - I just feel like I'm your average person. But, I'll do my best if you want to know anything!

Have a great day.

~Gaski

—

Well, a little about myself. I am graduating this semester from college! Before then, I was an Asian Studies major and I took three years of Japanese. Unfortunately, because of classes, I did not want to go an extra two years for Asian studies, so the quickest way out was in a double major. I had thoughts of going for Asian Studies for Grad school, and thought Journalism would benefit me highly.

I first came across [CENSORED] during my Asian Studies in my freshmen year. I watched one of your subs. At the same time, I was also doing research on [CENSORED] and his very strange, esoteric art. I later bought some of his books from Japanese book stores. I am surprised that nobody in the West knows about him. I have a good collection of his books. And sometimes, I feel like I should hire you to translate them for me, but I never get around it since I do my own translations.

Your [CENSORED] translations are good when anybody has the raw mangas.

I have to also say that I really love queer and eccentric art. I have always been an artist myself and I'm always looking to go into new mediums and discover new stuff. These days, I am a musician, writer, and video editor. I wish I had time to draw, but my drawings are expressed in my notebooks during class. I'm really looking to get a draw program editor thing so I can produce digital doodles.

Right now, I am actually writing a book due out in March and trying to promote it until then. So, I have been going on this podcast...

The book is about this strange subject called "Asian-Aryanism." Although I would like to share it with you, but for now, I think [CENSORED] will upload my show soon enough on his podcast. That way, there's a good introduction about myself on the show.

[CENSORED]... ...I think it's funny that you like Tsudo. I love him too. And every single character in [CENSORED] universe. I think [CENSORED] is quite controversial for Western audiences since he flirts with Yaoi, Pedophilia, some rape there, far-right imagery, some violence, esoteric imagery, quite confusing for any Westerner! This art is really only appreciated by some of the art world eccentrics. I really, really wish to see an official English translation of [CENSORED] and even the old-school anime in the West. I wish that world was real. [CENSORED] himself would be a queer artist by Western standards. All these strange underground artists just go into obscurity...

If you could be someone, would you be Tsudo? I dated, cuddle with, kissed, hugged, a transgendered person. And the funniest part was, she/he was scared to tell me she was originally born a guy! At first, it was a shocker, until I realized, I really liked her. And with this yaoi, I showed it to her... The relationship got better and we cuddled even more. ...I keep it a secret! Though we are good friends.

Always nice to talk to you!

-Steve P.

—

I don't update a ton usually, and there is one site where I never got to do anything. I had originally planned a webcomic, but the person I was going to work with flaked out right at the beginning, so I still have the domain but there's nothing there.

I generally keep most things about myself private. I don't use my real name online, but I go by both [CENSORED], though I mix them up often. I started taking Japanese at my community college because I needed to take a language and it was the only thing I was interested in. They offered two courses in Japanese. It was honestly pretty easy. I memorized the Hiragana and Katakana before the class started, and that got me through most of it.

After that, it was about three years before I got to university and took another Japanese course. In the meantime, I had picked up Silver Chaos and translated that. Those translations are still on my site, and if you look at them, that's what I did after taking beginner Japanese. For quite a while, I got up in the morning, turned on my radio station, and worked on Silver Chaos for a few hours before I drove to school, and that's how I kept my Japanese up while I didn't have any classes. I probably did that every day for about a year. By the time I did get into my next class, I had learned quite a bit on my own.

At some point, I saw a small article about [CENSORED]. As you can imagine, about 10+ years ago, there was barely any information at all about the series. I could hardly find anything on it. I didn't do anything about it right away. Like a lot of people, the art style was different and I wasn't used to it, and I wasn't sure about the series. At some point, and I can't say exactly what spurred it, but I just thought, "What the heck?" and imported about 80+ volumes from Japan. It was a pretty big expense, so I guess it was a major risk considering I might not have even liked the series.

I finished translating the first chapter in 2006. I guess that means I've literally been working on it for over ten years, since I didn't translate it in a day. I warmed up to it and, obviously, it ended up becoming a pretty big part of my life. Until recently, actually, I always translated a certain number of pages every single day. I even took it with me on vacation so I could keep working on it, never skipping a day.

I'd say a little over a week ago, I suspended my translations of [CENSORED]. Not because I dislike it or don't plan on doing it anymore, but because I received a job from a Japanese company that wanted me to work on the translations for their game, and I've taken the time I usually spend on [CENSORED] to work on that. It's a very big project, so it takes a lot of effort. It's practically my dream job :)

I usually keep personal info to myself, but since you brought it up, I will mention that I am transsexual. I don't post it to my stuff. I usually don't pick a gender if I don't have to on sites. If I do have to, I always pick male. There's still a lot of discrimination. People have assumed that I'm one or the other and I generally don't bother to correct them, so there's information about me calling myself both genders.

It's another part of the reason I'm a private person. People have done things like pretended to be fine with it so that they can 'get one over on me' later, mock and harass me. It's still a pretty cruel world out there, so I prefer to generally fly under the radar. I want people to see and enjoy my stuff, and it would be nice if some of my stuff made it big, but I don't necessarily want to be famous myself, you know?

~Gaski

—

Interesting.

I have to say something. [CENSORED] made me appreciate cross-dressers even more.

I flirted with the gay identity early in college to see where it would go. Really, I didn't think it was right for me and I couldn't find the pretty men I imagined I'd see. Or any platonic talkers into soft talking and kindness and… nice fun stuff. Like… the relationship of a parent and a child (I am geeky).

For a long time, my sexuality had been crushed by modern girls. And their whole world of selfishness. I first thought, "Well, this is the *wrong kind* of girl and it's just her as an individual." Until I slowly started to realize, all these same girls were wrong for me!

In fact, to some extent to my argument, it's all these preppy *white* girls that are bad.

And so, I slowly started to secretly read far-right stuff on the internet, what eventually would be known as the "alt-right." Although I do not associate with it now, I have many friends that are still into it.

…I have been to several WN events a couple of times…

I think F. Roger Devlin's *Sexual Utopia in Power* sums up all the bad white girls I dated. I got to meet the guy in person. But the fact of the matter is… the thing is… I am **NOT** a white nationalist. Once again, I am flirting with it.

I am quite young. This might sound somewhat crazy. But I didn't awake to this fact until last year. This whole time, since I was about 14, the best relationships I had were with Asian girls. And I used to think to myself, "they are just average people like white girls." And then I slowly started to realize… no they are not.

I prefer to date and have sexual preference for Asian girls! I was in denial about this before. And especially going to white nationalism was a bigger denial about my own self! The last WN event too… I had to bring my Chinese girlfriend. She was the only girl in the room and I was the only person with a girl to bring. Everybody was a serious male talking about the future and how everything is degenerate and bad. Now, my girlfriend did not shun me for such a belief. She loved me even more that I cared about my own people and wanted to get rid of things which were a bad influence. But the thing was... I loved her. And the relationship got even more intense and amazing. And now I realize I would like to take Asian Studies for grad school or pursue something similar.

I am writing a book on the subject of this White-Male Asian-Female phenomenon. Some of them said to me, even on this [CENSORED], that I "don't know what I am doing" or it is "a phase in my life," but the problem is, it's not and it's close to the truth about myself.

I did experiment with loving a transgendered person I told you. We are still good friends and sometimes he Snapchats me to go hang out and cuddle... but I have growing responsibilities and I would like to pursue... this might sound really controversial... I want an Asian wife and be in harmony with her family. I have never thought about things before when I first discovered Asian religion and culture. I feel better about myself now.

But yes, I take pride in the attitude that I am an eccentric artist and know things which would harm a Chinese relationship. I am trying to be a better person. But this love for Asian women and culture has always made me a better person. I am just trying to write a book about it.

The art of [CENSORED], and some other shojo artists I know about, define this type of Asian-White culture in art. I can't explain it in full detail, but it's there!

-Steve P.

***

Why I'm an Identitarian, by Steven Pronoko

"I have great respect for the East Asian races. Even if we were to go extinct, they could carry something on. They are by nature very racist and could be great allies of the White race. I am not opposed at all to allies with the Northeast Asian races."

-Dylann Roof

"If I had a son, he would look like Dylann Roof."

-Dr. Greg Johnson

"Summer bled of Eden

Easter's heir uncrowns

Another destiny lies leeched

Upon the ground

...Everybody needs someone to live by...

Rage on omnipotent."

-Talk Talk, Eden.

"True beauty is something that attacks, overpowers, robs, and finally destroys."

-Yukio Mishima

Who am I?

I come from a family with old money. My grandfather was an alcoholic and so is my father. We have a nice house in the bourgeois suburbs. I don't drink alcohol or do drugs, and I don't plan on it.

In elementary school, I was labeled "retarded" and kept away from kids at recess. This is typical of public school, after all. I was kicked out of the wrestling team for punching a kid who called me gay. Eventually, I was kicked out of high school because a gang of blacks heckled me and I fought back in self-defense. It's considered a "hate-crime" to do that. I was briefly sent to a special school. My parents then found an expensive private high school and saved me. Both the boys and girls in this school wore uniforms and were separated. I got the diploma. Now I'm in college.

I have dark feelings of repressed revenge and sexual masochism about high school. I want to hurt rich boys who ignored me and rape blonde girls who refused to acknowledge me. I really wanted to shoot up my school. Unfortunately, I said it on Twitter and went to court for it. I got off the case and pleaded that it was out of "pure ignorance."

I kissed a few guys out of kindness. The only boyfriend I had was a cute Thai kid. We started out as friends, then it turned to hugs, and then it became a pleasure to drive him home from classes. It went downhill after I kissed him. He didn't want to see me again.

I only had sex once. It changed my sexuality for good. The first time I masturbated was in the 6th grade and I thought about a cute Chinese girl that sat next to me. My first girlfriend was Chinese. The first time I ever kissed a girl was outside a movie theater. She was apparently Chinese too. And the first time I had sex was with a cute, nerdy Chinese girl at her dorm room. My current girlfriend is Chinese. I plan on proposing to her. You see, I unfortunately never had a proper relationship with a White girl.

Some would say I am experiencing an existential crisis. Why would I prefer Chinese women over my own kin? I have tried to find honesty in White women. They say they are beautiful, caring, and sexy. I hope white nationalists don't find White women attractive because of this. The truth is that White women are, by today's standards, naturally bourgeois and spoiled. It took me some time to understand this truth. It becomes obvious once you see it. White women should learn from Chinese women. White men know this too. It's why White culture is being surrogated in the wombs of the Chinese.

There is a common belief that Whites who date "Asians" are a part of one universal family. However, Whites who date Japanese *hate* Whites who date Chinese. I experienced this myself in the Asian Studies division. Compare and contrast a college-age Chinese-American club to a Japanese-American club. It's really a rivalry of Whites, who prefer the company of Chinese, versus the Whites who prefer the company of Chinese. The "Asian" terminology is flawed. Expect the formation of two parties of Pan-European Chinese and Japanese in the future. According to liberals, they will always be called "Multiracial." But according to White Nationalists, they will always be called a mistake. Will European brotherhood accept their biracial step-brothers? Unfortunately, the popular answer is no.

My love for Identitarianism is not based upon arrogance. It's about something deeper than that. If I could put it in a single sentence, *it's a theory about denying modernity and fighting for what is good and innocent*. It's also an "underground" thing too. Ironically, I only call myself a white nationalist just to piss people off. Much of the scene is filled with misfits and punks. White nationalism is the only authentic ideology for hipsters. Yet, there is this orthodoxy found on online comment boards. The typical and hilarious principles believed in the white nationalist scene is as follows:

- Excessive ethnocentric egotism is good.

- Whites must aggressively fight for an "Ethnostate" of some kind.

- Any system is good so as long White people are behind it.

- Sexual desire should be exclusive for the White woman.

- Having "hybrid" children is amoral.

- You're Jewish if you provide anything unorthodox to the movement.

Again, ask a white nationalist what he desires sexually and he will most likely argue for his beautiful, caring, sexy White woman. When tempted to fall for a foreign beauty, he will stubbornly deny his sexuality. White nationalists care too much for ideology and become absolute prudes.

Being an Identitarian means fighting for *your* identity. My identity belongs to only me. No one can tell you not to be an Identitarian. Those who enforce the law are submissive. White nationalism relies on wolves and sheep. An Identitarian already has his destiny planned out.

I will propose a controversial statement. I identify with everything that causes pain. There are five things that cannot be talked about in modernity. These things are about race, sexuality, IQ, class, and violence. Consider these classic conundrums:

- Why can't we call black people niggers anymore?

- Why can't we have sexual desires for children?

- Why can't mentally retarded people have the opportunity to become The President?

- Why does Molly get to study Japanese in Tokyo and Monica at her community college in Kansas?

- Why can't I have the right to kill somebody and get away with it?

This list is considered "immoral" and forbidden by thought. Someone will get offended. It causes a sort of pain. It's evil, they say.

Well, white nationalism is associated with all the above. Anything to do with the political Right has been pushed down so far, so no sympathy for the movement can occur. Ever since 1789, we have divided our family to be either associated with the Left or the Right. The Left represents egalitarianism, that all human beings are the same. The Right represents inegalitarianism, or that human beings are a part of nature. It was the Left that started The French Revolution and it is the Right that has been struggling since.

Most White people believe in egalitarianism. This is sometimes called "Progress." It is supposedly considered to be a good. But to be associated with the old world, or the

Right, is evil. Only criminals would be able to exploit race, sexuality, IQ, class and violence. You might be one of these freaks:

- Are you a racist skinhead?

- Are you a pedophile?

- Are you a mad scientist based on objective truth?

- Are you a corrupt politician?

- Or are you a cold-blooded serial killer?

...All these things are now associated with the Right.

White nationalists try so hard to be good. In other words, they try so hard not to be Jewish! Let's face it though, Western Civilization has strong ties with Judeo-Christian values. White nationalists believe they are normal, but normal people want white nationalists to be evil. It would further make sense that the biggest divide in the white nationalist movement is between the feelings of good and evil. Should white nationalists be good citizens and praise *American Renaissance*, or should they be evil Nazis that post offensive comments on *The Daily Stormer*?

I have good news. The postmodern age is still preaching without any meaning. The swastika is becoming ironic. The only obstacle now is morality. It's a dirty pleasure to be associated with the Right because it's both good and evil at the same time. Maybe some of us read both *American Renaissance* and *The Daily Stormer*. It's a theory about denying modernity and fighting for what is good and innocent.

The word "identitarian"is politically-correct. It's not rude like "white nationalist." I, however, enjoy my career as a thought-criminal. I don't have to serve a greater good for the white race. I can love my Chinese girl and support the cause for my own people. I don't care what anyone has to say about my own errors. All I have to do is be myself. It's everything who I am. I wish to strive for a good innocent life for my family and children. There is nothing better than to live a life of honesty, courage, integrity, and love. Freedom is a false concept. Modernity is against nature. We are animals ready to resist it. I breathe, therefore, I am. It's why I am an Identitarian.

Does it sound more exciting to become an Identitarian now? I will conclude with a semi-offensive Adolf Hitler inspired speech...

Identitarian! Listen! Read Yukio Mishima, Peter Sotos, Jim Goad, Colin Wilson, Bill Hopkins, Jonathan Bowden, Knut Hamsum, Sade and Céline!

Embrace race, sexuality, intelligence, class, and violence!

Start an enlightenment for criminals in a world of hypocrisy!

Avoid deconstructionism, any mainstream movie, and cultural rotting influences. It's about saving innocence, not harming it!

Embrace the feeling of anger, of gore, of ultimate experiences of which civilization is corrupting you! Let it out!

Embrace both submission and power!

Become the new barbarian!

...I took off my shoes before I entered the room to write this.

-S.P.

>:O

...There are three kids outside Upper Chestnut Elementary school. Donnie, Jake, and Tyler. Donnie has a stick and is chasing Jake and Tyler around.

"I'm going to get you Idiot-morons!"

"You can never crush an imbecile, imbecile!"

"Say that again and you're mince-meat."

This is the typical stuff little kids do when they make up an imaginary game. Say things right out of a Saturday morning cartoon dialogue. The kids are chasing around the "4-square" yellow imprint. Then little Monica came over.

"What are you guys doing?"

"Get out of the way, are you in it too?" Donnie says.

"I'm not in it!"

"Yes, you are!"

"I can't be! I am the jester! Ha-ha! Hear me out you dumb peasants! I am the best!"

"Here we go again...", Jake says.

Donnie with the stick says, "If you're not going to get in, then get out!"

Monica retorts back, "I am always in playing four square. Always in, always out!"

Monica went about making a stupid face and sticking out her tongue. Tyler noticed her silly dancing moves. He could

61

only think of it as like a penguin. Penguins are Tyler's favorite animal. And Monica acting like one made it all too real. Tyler watched her for a bit.

He said, "What's a stupid penguin like you dancing around here?"

"Me? I'm a Jester!"

Donnie reached out with his stick and poked Tyler with it. "Caught you! You're out! You're out!" Donnie and Jake laughed.

"Come get us if you can," Jake said as they both ran out. Tyler didn't feel the need to run after them for some reason. He just wasn't interested. He was too busy trying to convince Monica that she was a penguin!

"You are a Penguin! What makes you think you're not?"

"Well, does a penguin go like this? Quack Quack!" She quacked all the way.

"I'm going to get you!" Tyler yelled. "No!", Monica laughed.

Monica ran past a few dumb kids sitting on the ground. Tyler pursued her. He stepped over them anyway. Monica always ran to the big tree that was out of the playground's limits. It came close to that of a forest. Still, teachers could see kids from a distance. If the whistle blew at all and if there were any of them there. Monica liked to run around that tree multiple times. In circles. Looping. And soon enough, Monica was quacking while Tyler was chasing after her around and around that tree.

"No, no, no! You don't deserve to get me!" Monica fell to the ground.

"Why can't I get you?"
"You will never be the funniest jester as I am!"

"Why not?"

"Because you never will. And you wasted your whole time chasing me."

"Well I got you!"

Tyler pointed at Monica while she was sitting beside the big tree.

"Ok, yeah sure, you win!"

"What do I win?"

"Nothing."

Nothing!?"

"Nope, nothing!"

"That's unfair! I got you thought!"

"That still doesn't make you a jester."

"I hate jesters anyway."

"You liar, you hate jesters?"

"Yes, I do!"

"No, you don't!"

"Yes, I do!"

"Well how can I not be a jester?"

Monica looked around a bit. Confused and silly.

"Well you have to marry me." she said.

"What!? Marry you? No way."

"Yep! You're going to have to buy me a house. And a car…"

"No!"

"And have babies?"

"Babies!"

"Yes, and lots of babies! Tyler Jr. and Monica Jr., and…"

"No! No! No!"

"Yes! Yes!"

"Why does it have to be me?"

"Because you're a dog and dogs are only good for being one."

"A dog you say?"

"Yes! You're a big dog!" Monica chuckled.

"A big dog you say? Well I got news for you! I am a dog!" Tyler said.

"Oh really?"

"I'm a big dog. A really big dog!"

Tyler was jumping up and down. But this time, he had to show her something.

"Take a look at this."

Tyler zipped down his pants and held out his little penis.

Holding his penis, he said, "I'm a big dog, a really big dog!"

Dancing along with it like a little goblin.

Monica said "ewww!" And starting bursting out loud in laughter.

Tyler starting smacking his dick side to side.
"I think I'm going to need a bigger box! A bigger box for this dog!"

Tyler was wiggling it now.

"Your wee-wee is a dog!"

"Yes it is! And it's your dog now!"

Still laughing, Monica said "No way I'm going to be married to your wee-wee!"

"You're going to love my big ol' wee-wee!"

Monica was dying with laughter. Sitting under that tree.
Tyler flashing himself to a girl for the first time in his life.
The whistle blew. Everyone was lining up.
Still, Tyler and Monica were laughing under that tree.
Tyler was moving in closer to Monica.

"Get that doggie away from me!" Monica said while getting up.

She pushed Tyler's penis aside. Her five fingers spreading out like a star, smashing right into his testicles and his little forehead coming in between her middle finger.

"Bark Bark Bark!" he said.

"Put that doggie away before he gets everyone in trouble!"

Tyler was panting like a dog.

***

…It was a dark and stormy night. …So, they said about the life of Paul Clifford. But this night was actually raining. A storm would probably happen later on. No sign of it now.

The place was Shoemaker market. A strip mall of tiny storefronts ranging from "The Mighty Pawn" to some Hindi supermarket. It was closed at this hour. A car pulled up in the parking lot. Waiting for someone.

Tyler and Monica were in the car. Tyler was driving. Monica besides him. Tyler, holding his hands on the car's steering wheel, stayed silent for a bit. The car was parked. He turned off the car. Tyler looked down and gave a big sigh.

"Monica, I had so much fun tonight. I'm so happy we can see each other again. You're like the same person I knew when we were little."

"Thank you Tyler. You're a really nice person too," Monica smiled.

Monica looked at Tyler, and Tyler back at her. Monica this time wore really geeky, 70s style glasses. This is in a time where it was obviously not the 70s, but she wore them anyway because her eyes are small to begin with. Chinese girls get away with a lot of things that white people find outdated. And Tyler shaved yesterday, and it was that time of night where his five-o'clock shadow was starting to grow back, giving him the look of a handsome actor. Tyler smiled.

"You're such a funny person too."

"Thank you, I mean, I don't know what to say."

"Will you be ok this week?" Tyler said in an anxious tone.

"Don't worry again! I will. I just have work to do and I know Dad's kind of controlling and all."

"I hope it does not make your day sad."

"It doesn't."

Tyler went into Monica's chest for a seatbelt hug. Looking into her eyes too. And she did too.

"Ummm… high five!" Monica said.

Both smacked their hands in the air.

"Alright!" Tyler found it amusing.

"Just like old times," she said.

"Yeah, just like old times," he said.

This time, both smiled at each other with happiness. And this time, it was a long stare. Monica looked down at his unwashed black hair. Messy and string like. And Tyler used his nose to touch her forehead. Tyler could not help but to give her a little kiss between her eyebrows. "You're so nice," he said. She looked up this time. And she closed her eyes. He saw it coming. This time, a kiss on the lips. She moved back. He saw her open eyes. Both smiling. And now, he was moving in. Another kiss. Now getting really close. And in that exchange of kisses, Tyler's tongue reached inside Monica's mouth. Really slow, really soft. Very quiet. His arms slowly moved behind her back. And Monica put her arms on his stomach. This situation… a soft and mellow comfort zone. No one was outside to watch them kissing and the rain kept everything at ease. They kissed for two minutes. Slowly, Tyler raised his head over Monica. His knees reached over to her side, his butt no longer in the driver's seat.

"Monica, do you love me?"

Her nose on his cheek, "I do."

A little bump was in Tyler's pants.

"I'm really excited," Tyler said.

"Really?"

"Yeah."

Both looked down at that thing.

Tyler is shy. He shook his pants a bit.

"I want to see it," Monica said while she smiled.

"Uh, Ok. ...I guess."

Tyler slowly tried to pull down his pants, but was embarrassed to take it out. He'd never been in a situation like this before.

"Hold on, hold on."

Suddenly, Monica grabbed his lower underwear and his penis flicked out like a rubber pencil.

It was out in a really awkward situation. Monica still had a smile on her face.

"Haha," Monica chuckled.

Tyler said nothing. He was rushing with blood and scared at the same time. A traumatic movement was developing. Monica smiled. She touched the forehead with her finger.

"Wow. It looks like… a dog."

"What!?" Tyler said amused.

Monica laughed.

"I don't know."

Monica looked up at him.

"Your face, and then this thing, ha, doesn't look like you. It looks like some ugly little thing," she said."
"Uh, are you saying it's not normal… is it big?"
"No. You have a dog penis! Yes, you do! Haha."

Monica began patting Tyler's penis.

It stiffened, and was growing harder.

"Yes," Tyler said.

Monica was looking at his penis like it was a good friend she'd met before.

"Umm, should I...I'll...do it."

Tyler put his fingers around the shaft and started to go up and down.

Monica was laughing.

"The doggie is out! Hold on, I know what to do."

Monica swished her hand, moving Tyler's off his penis, and she took over. She began slightly jerking Tyler off.

"How's the doggie now?'", she said.

"Ha," Tyler made a bleep.

He began looking left and right to see if anyone was outside, even her dad was to come along. It was not like the whistle was going to blow anytime soon.

All of a sudden, Monica was acting like a little kid. Tyler put his hands around Monica's shoulders. He was quiet as he obeyed Monica's command. Tyler turned into a cow being milked by a farmer. Red in his face.

Monica was stroking the dog penis. Like she was a little kid waiting for something to come out of it. She was excising a power she hadn't done before, but had dreamed about through the hentai she watched and the yaoi manga she read. She wasn't even Japanese and knew little Chinese.

Her mom and dad spoke it, and disciplined her by the old Confucius ways. And she would lock herself in her little bedroom, surfing the internet, creating fake identities, and talking to far-away people online. Until she found Tyler again.

She didn't even need to wear her thick Ray Ban glasses to look at it. It just made her look sexy at this point. Like an angry and ugly Chinese nerd trying to ace her chemistry exam. That's what she was anyway. The person she grew up to be. But she was enjoying, with a smile on her face. The other types like her can't even make a smile, but look sexy anyway. She at least was showing happiness.

Monica was shafting it hard this time. Tyler felt something.

"Thank you Monica, thank you, …I love you," Tyler moaned.

She kept a smile on her face. She was happy too but didn't have the words to say it.

Monica slowed down a bit.

"Should I get it out now?" Tyler said.

"No, hold on."

Monica changed the jerking with her right arm. She could get more pressure on it. She was on full speed this time. The penis was red. Blood going through Tyler. It was about to happen.

"Monica, ohhhh Monica! It's happening!"

"Doggie, doggie!" She said like a little kid.

"Oh…"

Tyler was watching Monica the whole time she jerked him off. His memory already scarred. This is the moment in his life that he would always remember. The moment in his life that he wished he could live over and over again. The moment in his life that was meaningful to his existence.

"Monica," Tyler said. "The little things are going to come out."

"What things?" Monica purposely played dumb.

"My little Tyler's," he laughed. "And… they are going to land on you."

To land on Monica without a womb.

"Ok! Come out then!" she said.

Stroking, and stroking. Boiling up.

"Ahhh."

And then some little liquid came out. Monica lowered the penis. A slow little white flood. And then, a shot. Right on Monica's shirt. A few more shots. Monica lowered it to see the sperm come out.

"Ohh… Ahh. Oh, oh. oh. Oh."

Monica laughing as it came all over her.

Some sperm now on her jerking hand.

Tyler now panting like a dog he is.

The car heating up like in the summer.

Monica was all messy. She looked at her hand.

"You got it on me!" She said. "The little Tylers are on me!"
She wiped her spermy hand on her pants.

"Monica… I love you." Tyler reached down for kisses on
the cheek.

Kissing. Kissing passionately.

A little rushed? Yeah. Too quick for a kiss when she still
has sperm on her.

Tyler looked down at Monica.

The sperm, the little Tyler's, sliding down her cute Hello
Kitty shirt. Like a waxed candle.

Monica giggling. She was wiping it off.

"It's all over me now."

"I love you Monica," Tyler smiled.

Panting. Panting like a dog.

Looking down on it. What has he done? A dog that missed the womb. And the children lay dying.

But both were blushing. A happy feeling. His first girl, her first boy.

"Is it dried up now?" She looked at his penis.
Tyler did not know what to say. He started pulling up his pants. He went in for a cuddle.

Monica. She was thinking. Daydreaming.

A few minutes later, a buzzer from her phone. Her dad was here. Somewhere behind them in the rainy parking lot.

"I have to go," she said.

"Ok. See you next time…. Bye," he said.

"Bye."

"I love you."

"I love you too."

A kiss.

Monica walked out of Tyler's car into the rain. She quickly ran into her father's car. She took the front seat while her Dad drove home.

"How was tonight?" he would probably say.

"Good, nothing much."

And the sperm, still on her clothes like drippings of the rain. And a little white spot under her wrist. The whole time in the car with her dad. She liked it. Knowing that Tyler's children were taking a ride on her the whole time tonight, until they died and shriveled up into nothing. Knowing that Tyler owned her. She was his dog.

***

A list of comments selected from 4 Reasons You Shouldn't Date Asian Girls by Clear Above.

(http://therightstuff.biz/2016/02/03/4-reasons-why-you-shouldnt-date-asian-girls/)

asiansexual
A rare sexual dysfunction that cause the sufferer to only go after people's of a preferred gender from China, Japan, Korea (All three are referred to as the "Big Three", like car companies.), Vietnam, or the Phillipines. Males hailing from the state of California are a majority of sufferers, though anyone from anywhere can have it. The most perplexing thing is that the root cause in still unknown, and scientists aren't really out for the answer, as it's apparently not all that high on their priority lists. However, it is doubtful that one is born being an asiansexual.

To put that in plain, everyday english for the simplest human to understand: Being an asiansexual means, in a nutshell, to only want an asian as a boyfriend/girlfriend/ sexual partner exclusively, and to think that people of other ethnic backgrounds just don't quite cut it anymore, if they ever have at all in the first place. To prefer asians, but still like white girls is not being asiansexual. It's when you exclude other peoples in your hunt for the perfect mate. An epidemic, or just a preference taken too far? Strange, or normal like the blue sky? Racist, or reasonable? I'll leave that for you, the reader, to decide.

Paul Kisling • a month ago
I prefer dating Asians, Indians/Middle Eastern, or Western Europeans. I avoid entitled western women like the plague to the point I haven't banged one in 15 years. Just not worth

the drama/cost and upkeep. The mere thought of a doing so makes me nauseous with angst.

<u>謝鈺和</u> • <u>2 months ago</u>

I seriously suspect that you all have double standards. I am an Asian man living in Taiwan, and My girlfriend is Hungarian. But this is the case mainly because I can't find any Asian girl who is brave and intellectual enough to think and feel and live their life not affected by white aesthetic standard and materialism. I do agree with many of you that many Asian women regard white males as a status symbol and are gold diggers, but why do you think that's so very commonplace in our culture? Who came here with military might in 19th century to shovel in our throat materialism, and who is continue doing so by manipulating us with all those propaganda based on psychological action set off by Freud?? Imagine you grow up in a social-political setting in which all references to "success"and "beautiful" are mostly all associated with white people, AND YOU CAN'T AVOID SEEING THEM AROUND YOU, you think you wouldn't be affected by it?? No one is born to be shallow and racist, and the implications of environment shouldn't be ignored. Please kindly all hold your tongue back when you criticize others, calling Asian women whores or bitches, before doing some serious research in history.

Peace.

<u>SouthOhioGipper</u> • <u>6 months ago</u>
Wow. Not only did I commit the sin of being with an Asian woman. I married an Islamic Asian woman. Guess I just cucked out. Oh well, too bad for the white race. My kids speak 3 languages and can travel and fit in just about anywhere on planet earth. I think their options are better than most white kids stuck in an Appalachian trailer park.

But you enjoy all that racial purity while I go mix my genes with a descendant of the Khans. Real conquerors.

Daniel Hart • 6 months ago
I personally don't give a fuck who marries who. Getting married and having children should not be forced on people. It should always be optional. People can either choose to do it or not. Me, personally, I'd rather be single until I die. Marriage nowadays is a raw deal for guys anyway. In case of a divorce, the outcome usually favors women more. A man can end up losing his house, his cars, half his money and a bunch of other valuables. The ex-wife gets half of his stuff. Fuck that shit. I'm not going to risk losing half of my things I worked really hard for to a fucking greedy materialistic gold digging cunt. So, if some people out there are planning to get married and have kids someday, fine by me. Go ahead and do it. I don't care if you marry someone of your own race or another race and fuck this article that's obviously been written by an irrational racist white supremacist Nazi KKK piece of shit coward. FUCK YOU!!!!

Damian Ray • 6 months ago
This article is a fucking joke, I'm 1/4 Asian, my father is Asian and white and we are both normal and contribute well in society, who ever wrote this article must be trolling or has yellow fever himself but can't get one or some jealous white girl who most likely lost a man to an Asian chick, smfh

Sacco Vandal • 9 months ago
In the Corps I was stationed in Okinawa Japan for 3 years. Slept with and dated a lot of Japanese girls that time, even considered marrying one and staying in Japan. One thing stopped me: I had this deep instinctual desire FOR MY

CHILDREN TO LOOK LIKE ME. I now have 3 beautiful. blond-haired, blue-eyed Aryan children.

Asian women are great, but if you want white babies you have to mate with a white woman, it's that simple.

George Williams • 9 months ago
In the US if a white and black marry, their offspring will be considered black, even if they subsequently marry whites - for generations - due to the one-drop rule legacy. While such a union may actually confer genetic benefits such as hybrid vigor, the offspring will be burdened by social/ cultural liabilities as long as this country retains its covert prejudices, so there is a pragmatic reason to marry within race.

Asians don't share this burden and the Asian appearance typically dilutes in a couple of generation. But your Asian (Chinese) wife may be a "Tiger Mom" who will visit psychological issues on your kids with her militant rigor in their education, and her parents will be looking over your shoulder in case you aren't measuring up yourself. A reason is that most Asians here are a self-selected group of highly motivated, intelligent and often well educated people or else they wouldn't have taken the risks and disruptions to come here in the first place.

GermanicConfederate • 9 months ago
I like Asian people, in general, and I find Asian women attractive but I wouldn't consider them girlfriend or wife material. I love that my little bastards look like me and have so many mannerisms common to my family line. :

Ezra Pound • 9 months ago
I thought "Asian Fever" was more of a joke. I didn't realize it was actually a real thing on the Alt-Right.

Fugio Penny • 9 months ago
I guess I'm a lucky half breed. I'm half Japanese, half Irish.
6 foot 3, reasonably well built and in good health (plot twist
is my dad was a big Japanese dude, mom is the daughter of
Irish immigrants. Hopefully this gives me some sort of
protective shield here because something something Jared
Taylor Japanese something something). I grew up
completely around the white side of my family and was
raised Catholic. I'm proud of all those heritages but feel
strongly and primarily American, and have never had any
identity crisis to speak of (unless the usual high school
punk rock phase counts).

I lived in China for some years and during that time had a
snow white Scandinavian girlfriend. That combo turns the
local ladies' knees to noodles. Status off the charts. I'd be
happy to see America become more WASPy, just leave
room for us mongrels to have some fun on the sidelines!

Laguna Beach Fogey • 9 months ago
White men with Asian fetishes should be banned from
attending the upcoming **National Policy Institute (NPI)**
and **American Renaissance (AmRen)** conferences.

No degenerates!

Cobbett • 9 months ago
I prefer Pattaya bar girls(and SE Asian women in generall)
to what's on offer regarding English women these days, not
that I'm looking for a 'meaningful' relationship either
way...and don't particularly care what anyone thinks of it.

Laguna Beach Fogey • 9 months ago
I can't stand Asian females myself--they look like aliens--
but they certainly love me. Must be the tall Viking
physique, beard, and blue eyes.

Asian chicks are some of the fattest, most materialistic, most entitled females out there. What self-respecting White man would go with one?

These days I'm seeing a lot more White girls with Asian boys, than White men with Asian girls. It's a weird trend. I've even noticed an example or two of this on television.

This past weekend we spotted a normal-looking young White dude with a chubby Asian girl. I thought, WTF?! He could do much better. I still see the occasional White guy with an Asian wife and ugly half-breed children, which always makes me react in disgust. These men don't know how ridiculous they look.

JosephtheGreat • 9 months ago
I have nieces that are half Asian but they are all girls so I don't think they will grow up to be an Elliot Rodger. I just have to make sure they don't become alcoholics. But it makes me feel kinda bad to be here now. I mean I'd kill to protect my nieces. Just so I'm straight here: We're only going to gas the jews, right?

JosephtheGreat Goys in the Hood • 9 months ago
My nieces like to think of themselves as white. Once when my niece was five we asked her what her race was and she said "I'm half asian and half normal." We all laughed really hard.

fish.heads • 9 months ago
How about reproducing with White/Asian mixed race girls to dilute the oriental out? I'm sure in a few generations you'd be down to at least Finnish levels.

Laguna Beach Fogey • 9 months ago
The Asian Fever on the Alt-Right is mostly limited to the virgin spergs, autistics, and beta-boy incels who hate Roissy and Roosh.

keithmahone • 9 months ago
Why are there temptations: White women tend to be picky, balky, confused and very disloyal (thanks to several generations of Cultural Marxist programming by Jews). A white man is naturally attracted to women who have not had their gender role de-natured by a Sexual (read: Satanic Jewish) Revolution. That being said, I've never dated outside my race. And in Northern Virginia at least, the standard of living for Asian women is much, much higher than the average American. They would never settle for a guy just being White.

Uncle Adolf • 9 months ago
The idea of marriage/dating based on romantic love (finding your "soul mate," regardless of religion, race or now even sex) is relatively new. For centuries, marriage was an economic arrangement between families.
If you're really serious about "revolting against the modern world," you should start by rejecting one of its core ideas: romantic love.

The_Legend_Ron_Jeremy Nicole Black • 9 months ago

"Who could ever marry a female gook?"

The only people who *wouldn't* want to marry a female gook are Gay men and most white fascists -- but I repeat myself. (picture of beautiful Chinese woman)

Liberal Juggalo supremacist The_Legend_Ron_Jeremy • 9 months ago

83

Asian women are the last step before coming out as gay. Everyone knows that.

DenisetheCelt • 9 months ago
Fellas - your little China Doll turns into the Dragon Lady, the moment they get that ring on their finger. They are, by nature, infinitely more materialistic than White women, and I knew a great big Puerto Rican "macho" man, who was married to an Asian woman. He was big, aggressive and muscular - but she turned him into the most subjugated Cuck I EVER met in my life, We got into a fight once, because the yellow bitch from Hell said that my fellow parked in "her" parking space. My guy was a quiet fellow, and I am a Celt, so I went at it with that SKANK. I scared the HELL out of her, because Orcs are NOT used to Whites fighting back. I ran into her man, a few days later, He started to get aggro, and defend her - and I cut him short, and told him the entire thing was her fault, He didn't fight back at all. His great big shoulder sunk, and his head dropped, and he muttered an apology. I couldn't believe it. I was used to cocky, combative PR's. If you want to be an Uber henpecked Cuck - marry Yellow.

Batlord • 9 months ago
I would honestly hope no alt-rightists would seriously consider having mixed race children with an Asian woman. I'd also hope we'd all have the moral character to not be going looking for casual sex, with Asian women or otherwise. Also, this infatuation some guys in our circles seem to have with Eastern European women seems like basically the equivalent of yellow fever within the microcosm of the alt right.

Dave6034 • 9 months ago
Don't dismiss the genetic angle just because it's politically incorrect. There's enough genetic distance between Whites

and Asians, and enough dysfunction in their hybrids, to justify classifying them as different species. We're not cousins whose ancestors yesterday walked out of Africa, but distinct branches of the hominid tree that independently evolved intelligence to survive in similar but widely separated climate zones.

Notice how Asians score about equal to Whites on IQ tests, but are vastly less capable of original thinking. E.g. "Kung-fu Panda" consisted entirely of Chinese cultural elements and was wildly popular in China, yet only white Americans would think of making such a movie. Different brains regulated by different genes.

Hybrids are messed up not because their parents are self-hating racists, but because their brains, like their faces, are an incoherent mix-up of White and Asian features. It's like having a race riot inside your head!

(...Atari Teenage Riot anyone? -pilleater)

TruthSeeker • 9 months ago
Back in my liberal, blue-pilled, and fat days I did date a couple of Asian women. And yea, to be perfectly honest, white women didn't like me back then. At all. I might as well have been invisible. I was maybe a 4 on the scale, the idea of getting even an average 6/10 white girl was a practical impossibility. But getting a 6/10 Asian girl was pretty normal and well within my range.

Even back then I knew I would never have children with an Asian girl. For one simple reason, they're fucking crazy. The more Americanized ones (aka the only ones you'll date) are some of the most batshit people I've ever met. Since losing the weight, I exclusively date white women however. Although I wouldn't say that many of them aren't also crazy, at least I relate to their experience.

Asian fever is a byproduct of three concurrent factors. One is that the white men who date Asians are generally losers who as a matter of fact cannot do that much better. The other is that Asian women compared to other minorities are much more likely to find things like intelligence attractive (aka your autism) because they tend to have higher IQs than other races. And lastly, Asian women because of higher IQs are much more likely to enjoy higher intellect pursuits (like higher level academic courses), therefore increasing exposure to high-intelligent, beta, white men.

Flavius Stilicho TruthSeeker • 9 months ago
I will tell my friend that his Japanese girlfriend loved him equally for his intelligence as for his...ahem.

Seriously, though, your account reflects the anecdotal accounts I heard from my friends who taught English in Japan.

TruthSeeker • 9 months ago
Asians have no intellectual curiosity, they only really study to advance themselves materially.

Jeff Haushofer • 9 months ago
Most white men who are into Dog-Eaters are wimps with latent paedo urges. Also, Oriental women are dull and have personalities of goldfish. Yeah, and apparently they have no pubes and their minges go sideways. It's true. I read about it in a book.

<u>Vlad Pepes</u> • <u>9 months ago</u>
Only by bedding down with Asian girls can the prophecy of
the Sperg Hybrid Master Race be fulfilled.

<u>Anti-Citizen</u> • <u>9 months ago</u>
Lets also stop pretending that most White guys with Asian
girlfriends don't get the equivalent of a mudshark. This is
especially valid for those who get them abroad, i.e.
Thailand, Philippines. The fact is that while these countries
make money out of sex tourism (aka pussy thirsty beta
males), most of the degeneracy is contained to certain cities
with the majority of the country remaining very traditional.
If a girl doesn't want to get disowned and shamed by her
family and entire village, she need to get a foreign man
who is rich and respectable, not some generic White weeb.

Another thing is that these women turn SJWs within a
couple of years once they come in contact with Western
society. You can see on college campuses how most Asian
girls are very dedicated fighters against white male
patriarchy or whatever, even proclaiming that they share
the same experience of oppression as Blacks and Latinos.

Thirdly, if you want to see the future you chose in term of
offsprings, you can go on /r/hapas/ and see that basket
cases there.

Grim • <u>9 months ago</u>
I have an Asian Girlfriend, and the reasons for that are
outlined above. White women seem vein to me and I have a
particular hate for the feminist scourge that affects them.
They are brought up as princesses and expect that their
whole life. They do very little to earn it, they actually think
men should earn every little thing. Most white women I
have dated never cooked me a single meal, never shared the
bill at a restaurant and well ... the sex is usually

disappointing at best. I do understand that that may not reflect the majority and I have just lucked out. I am a good looking guy though, tall, slim athletic from years of kickboxing. The problem with leaving her is I can't fault her. I get food for work, food when i get home, clothes are washed, house is clean... All I have to deal with is a pet rabbit. We have never had a "fight" all our arguments are resolved through rational compromise, and the sex.... hollyyy mother of god. BJs in the morning ... everything. For 2 years too... it hasn't slowed, its increased and I am the one turning sex down, and her response to that is initiating it in the morning when I can't think properly.

Do white girls like this exist? I would love to meet one. I would do everything for her.

dodoros • 9 months ago
Is it worth it to divorce an Asian girl so that you might have an opportunity to marry a normal white girl?

(The Birth of Prudence conundrum. -pilleater)

Todd Clemmer • 9 months ago
It's just too much Japanese anime and the desire to live it.

Bolo y Sombrero Todd Clemmer • 9 months ago
That explanation really doesn't work. Most anime characters look rather White to me. I've also noticed that a large number of Whites with Asian wives are not anything near anime fans. They are nerdy, Beta, but they're more of a wilting businessman/academic type than anything else.

Ragnar Blåskägg • 9 months ago
There is quite a lot of guys with yellow fever and half asian offspring in and around the alt right so this article is definitely relevant. Almost all white guys i have seen with asian women in real life were nerds though, nothing wrong with being a nerd but still...

Flavius Stilicho • 9 months ago
A good friend of mine taught English in Japan for a work term. His experience was that it was the spinsters (over-25 women) that would start dating Whites. The Japanese have a very high preference for their own race, and it's only the prospect of a daughter never getting married that would lead them to consider a White guy (but never a man from a Black or Brown race).

As a digression, his experience is that Japanese men are equally fearful of and enthralled with the idea of the "Big White Cock". He'd get invited to bathhouses for them to see if the myth was true (and no suggestion at all of homosexuality). In his words "I'm kind of average size here, but it was great for the ego walking through that bathhouse taking off my robe and letting it swing around."

Patriarchal Shitlord • 9 months ago
Wait, are you telling me that Asian women aren't all loyal cute 2D waifus who will never leave you? I don't believe you.

scythian Marcus Halberstram • 9 months ago
I have played Conquistador quite a bit. I can tell you Asian girls are the most neurotic and yes autistic in an antisocial way, They seem to go for a very particular type of white guy. The more Americanized types go for more brutish white guys but most Asian women like Betas with a salary. I never did well with Asians but killed it with every other

mystery meat variety of girl. Girls who are on the periphery of white value white features far more than white women. Blonde women have no attachment to blonde men. But Christian Lebanese/Syrian, Persian and mixed race South American Types have an overwhelming preference for white especially Nordic looking men. It's almost like they want to get the non Euro bred out of them. Once you get the Asian thing out of your system it ceases to be attractive. However I always have a soft spot for more Dark featured Caucasoid looking women. I suppose I enjoy being put on a pedestal which these women tend to do with fair haired light eyed men. That being said I tend to put blonde and red headed women on a pedestal. Which works against my efforts with them. Either way the only women I would reproduce with would be one that was genetically similar to me and could give me kids that looked like me. So for marriage its got to be a blonde.

Laguna Beach Fogey • 9 months ago
These days I see more White girls with Asian guys, than White guys with Asian girls.

WTF is going on?

***

Let's not "red-pill" the masses. Let's not make Laura say "Harambe" in an EDM dance club...

I never want to see Laura again.

I met her on some internet dating website. Yeah, she looked cute. And the campus was about three hours away from me. Maybe, just maybe, she would drive over here and we could meet in person. I would just have to woo her over through texting. It's fun that way.

Too bad I found out today she was a slut.

I hate Snapchat. She had a Snapchat and didn't even tell me. I thought I would re-introduce myself and be friends again. I haven't seen her in over two years. I got another Chinese girlfriend... until she broke up with me. She hates how I have The Turner Diaries on my bookshelf. That's not me! Well, her fault for breaking up. She is missing out.

My brother told me to get Snapchat. I thought I could make more friends that way. Improve friendships. Nope. The reverse effect came. The whole thing is a "Jealousy Window." I do not need that in my life. Already I am a loner. I have to get through college and continue my job at Home Depot. Who cares. I am going to grad school too. Undergrad is not enough. It's an embarrassing place. I don't want to go to my private college-on-the-hill which once was a girls' school, always a girls' school. They opened it up for men and men don't show. This school is going to scare me forever. And Snapchat is not helping my life any better.

Around December I will be free from this.

I thought it would be nice to show Laura I went to a New York Knicks game. Yeah. All good men go out with their

91

"bros" and enjoy a night at basketball. It's fun. Basketball reminds me so much of Chinese culture. I love basketball for those nostalgic reasons only.

I thought girls like Snaps. That's what my brother says anyway. Until I found out you can never get rid of it.

That's not me. I'm not a bro. I'm not a normie. I want to be myself. But this decadent, Jewish culture bombards every aspect of life. I couldn't be more blunt. Do Asian girls know about this too? Or do they play along with it? They really don't mean any of it. They chase after white boys because they are successful. And then when those Chinese girls hit 30, they come crawling back to Chinese males when they realize they were the ones with success and tradition. Western culture does delude the Chinese in this way.

Am I being used?

Ok, I think it's time to clearly write how I feel. What I witness through these... Snaps.

(I'm thinking about Andy Nowicki right now. Very depressing stuff about... game culture).

It was two days before Halloween, and you know, this year it's on a Monday. Everyone will celebrate it on a Friday this year (I won't). And Laura did.

And I saw her.

She dressed up as a native American Indian.

Cute, harmless. Totally something Milo would promote. She can get away with it because she's Chinese. I think.

Some cute photos with her Med student friends.

Those ugly slut white girls. I fucking hate face paint. It doesn't make them any prettier.

And then... the poses.

The tantalizing... The cute pictures with her and giving peace signs.

Not hippie like, totally Asian and hot.

And then, she got into this... dance club.

I refused by today's decadent culture. Why not go to church or board game club or see a concert or go to a cafe meeting or...

She said "Harambe" out loud. Just for 6 seconds in that club.

I fucking hate Harambe now. I don't fucking care if this is a joke against Black Lives Matters or why niggers are fucking stupid to begin with. I hate this post-postmodern world of extreme irony and sarcasm. A fucking white male can't even live a normal life without pretending to be some dispirit character on Adventure Time.

Is Laura like that? I hope not. I swear to god, I hope she is not.

It's why I don't want to see her again.

All these White-Male, Asian-Female couples. Their fucking Dario Šarić look-a-likes and fucking glass wearing hipshot girls.

When I was 22, I didn't play basketball. I was in Japan learning Japanese. And taking pride in all the SWPL things that came into my life. And I was aware of The Jewish Question™ too. I did not get a live audience. I wasn't a fascist like him. Why don't all these Alt-right people stop bitching and start lifting weights and getting drafted by the major leagues? Happy people shut up when they get everything on a silver platter. Paul Bingham said that somewhere… give everyone an Asian girlfriend. Yes. Please do. Make them shut up.

I am so glad I don't look like fucking Šarić.

If I was gay, I would fuck Šarić so hard. I think I have a crush on him.

Someone once said that yellow fever is the next step towards homosexuality. I would consider it.

Let's not "red-pill" the normie. I don't want to be normal. I am myself. Andy Nowicki is right.

Trauma at the moment. Can't think. Too stressed.

"They called it, 'Race-Play,'… 'This is really the sub-text of our entire relationship'… 'Yeah, you know, my girlfriend is Asian, and… sometimes I have her dress up like my China doll.'"

-Ryan Landry on BDSM, Red Ice Radio.

Race Play:

An avant-garde, but increasingly accepted form of sexual role play in which people of different races consensually reject all political correctness (especially verbal) and propriety in favor of sexual pleasure and fulfillment.

Q: (furtively) "You into race play at all?"
A: "Yeah, call me yo NIGGER APE - makes monkey's dick jump like crazy!"

-Urban Dictionary

by jamaica55 July 19, 2009

(http://www.urbandictionary.com/define.php?term=Race+Play&defid=4119738)

"Speaking of taboo kinks, this makes me wonder what people think of age play, too. (For those of you not aware of it, one person plays a child and the other one plays an adult who is molesting/abusing the child... sometimes there's an incest component to it as well—e.g., daddy/ daughter.) I've often wondered what draws people to such roles—I could see, for example, an incest/molestation/rape survivor taking on the child role in order to sort of reorganize her/his feelings about the past, finding it somehow empowering to be "in control" (if only via her/his consent in participating) in the sexual experience.

And like others have said about the race-play thing, I find myself a lot more able to empathize with the person taking the disempowered role than the person taking the powerful role. I'm not sure why that is."

-Professor Pink

"I'm the opposite - outside the bedroom, I'm an independent, strong, dominant type. But when it's just me and the mister, I want nothing more than to be thrown around like a ragdoll. It's a release. Same with people in your situation - being a dom/me would be an outlet for you.

When you find that right person, give it a try. I bet you'd be really good at it."

-brotherjo

...I remember that day. 18 years old. Nothing better to do. So, I took a walk on the train tracks being bored. I don't have a girlfriend or any guy friends to go hang out with. The first day of high school was hell. No one said hi to me, and I missed the bus back home. I walked back home crying for 40 minutes. Nobody wants me there at that shitty, bumfuck public school. What a way to ruin my early life! I had so much potential. I didn't know any better. And my parents didn't know anything better at all either. They thought they would just send me to school and I would magically make friends and shut-up.

And then when you don't have a car, and you're still in the 11th grade, 18 years old, and you know about crazy shit like William L. Pierce and a fan everything Crimethinc puts out... It gets to you. No one thinks like me. That is, if my family was rich and we lived in California. And then I would finally get to hang out with rich kids that think like me. That's the answer. And then liberals give us the internet to "liberate" our sense of meaning. Only to feel more isolated and alone than ever before.

You see, no one cared that my favorite bands were Atari Teenage Riot or KMFDM. I am the only kid to go to punk shows, like Realicide, and to actually see Merzbow in person.

"You're too young for that," those old washed out Gen-x teachers might say.

And my only "true friends" I consider, are the ones in elementary school and through Omegle.

I am not ashamed to use dating websites either. I have been using them since I was 16 and kept it a secret from my parents. And I get to meet these internet strangers in person.

But this girl, Laura, I met her online. And she is the only friend I can talk to.

I remember strolling along the train tracks by myself. No one with me. Why? I don't have a car. Besides, where would I drive to? There is nothing to do in the suburbs. It's cool. This place has a forest, a river, and a train complex. The trains make noise at night. Freight train actually. That's why living here is inexpensive. I'm used to the noise by the train track.

I remember kicking rocks and singing, *Kiss to Kiss* by Mako. A Eurobeat act. ...Dejo and Bratt Sinclaire. Classical. MAX does a wonderful cover of the song too. All those cute Japanese girls and singing this song back in the 90s. The time of their life.

"Kiss to Kiss, I love you. Kiss to Kiss, I need you. Kiss to Kiss, I'm losing myself."

Singing that slowly... while kicking rocks. Like I was Eeyore the donkey.

Once in a while, I will get a text from her. I need someone to talk to. I don't know if she knows I am in a different situation than her.

I remember this April Fools, I texted her... "bad news, my house burned down :(."

I played along with it the whole time! And all I got from her was "You're such a good friend! I care about you!"

Dragging it along, until I texted back an hour later, "April Fools :)."

She was shocked! I felt I'd planned a really good April Fools joke. Later, a few years later, I think the joke about how "my mother died," to Molly was the best one yet. But at the time, I wooed over Laura's heart and kept her attention through texting!

But anyway…

I think I was texting her about that day. I don't remember how exactly it went, but from my memory, it went something like this…

"Hey, are you busy with homework this week? (I always put on a facade about my own events and try to talk like I am ok, which is not true. This has haunted me in the long run with text relationships)."

"No, not really, I am watching TV in my dorm."

"Netflix?"

"Yes, I love… (That one anime, slipping from my mind. something to do with high-school swimmers)."

"I think I saw one episode. I like Slam Dunk."

"Oh? That one about basketball, that's an old one."

Now you can imagine this while I'm singing to myself, walking slowly home, with a big sigh. Depressing. Why do I do these things when other kids are taking drugs? I don't do drugs. The only drug I want is sex, and lots of it… If I can get any of it to begin with.

"And then there is (Other mainstream amines I could care less about. Not going to watch anytime soon. Never.)."

"Yeah, yeah, I have seen that one episode."

And we would talk like this back and forth until I didn't feel like texting back or she would fail to respond. That's the saddest part. When the conversation stops. It feels like we never talked in person. It was just little Victorian messages being sent here and there in the year 2009. Odd. My heart would drop. Once I get home, I cry in bed. I felt so aloof. I still do. That feeling comes back to me. Still I cry in bed.

No, I don't have depression and I don't enjoy crying. I feel like a loser. I feel like I could have ever been there on the train tracks with her. I'm really sad. I am not sure if that is actually quite possible… with her being two hours away. With no car.

Am I living that old Victorian period? This is probably what Goethe felt. No. He did feel this.

I ask myself, why must?… I…

...I remember her in my 8th grade English class.

She always looked upset and angry, and she was ugly too.

That is, I thought she was ugly.

Her eyebrows always slanted down. Her face was an oblong square. You couldn't even see her eyes. And how small she was, with her red sweater that made her look like an old grandma.

She would be silent all the time and diligent with her school work. I could never see her. I sat up front and had to deal with the nanny teacher.

"Well of course, my son and his wife are residing in Japan. He was in the military," the teacher would say.

I always thought to myself, "is his wife Japanese?"

Never so sure.

It was that same class, where I had to write down my favorite bands I like, and the teacher read each name aloud. I remember her slowly speaking, "Mouse on Mars, Placebo..." And the dorky kid in the corner laughing his ass off because he didn't know those were actual band names.

But it was that girl, who unfortunately I forgot her name, ...either it was Stephanie or Sarah, who just rolled her eyes and didn't laugh at all.

Yeah, she would do that. I used to think she was a heartless creature.

Then there was that other time, where I had to make a public speaking address. That gook-faced girl goes, "Oh no

Joe, don't go embarrassing me." She said it in a passive aggressive way.

My only thought was, "She's a brat. Who cares what she says?"

The speech was about the president of the Staples corporation. I made the speech powerful like he was the President of the USA. Everyone laughed when I got to the part about him being the President of a company no one really cared about.

I did these practical jokes like these because I wanted attention. I wanted this attention so that I could be respected for my sense of avant-garde humor. But ironically, I didn't know my own self. And I was told, like so many other kids, "to be yourself" and accept your own personal standards. My own standards were too bizarre and controversial for everyone else.

A big question, I like to think to myself, is that of my high school time. I rarely had any girl to go out on a date with. I was told that a girl would choose me, like a Sadie Hawkins dance. ...It only happened a few times, and at those times, I learned about the unstable nature of young people and confused girls.

I don't think I even improved on my dating skills since then. More men my age are looking up advice on Roosh V's website and studying the esoteric nature of Game. I first learned about Game when I was 20. I thought it was a shocker, and still find the stuff easily offensive. Five years later, I am still that same person.

I will be honest. Recently, I was making out with my girlfriend on the beach.

I received four different blowjobs in my life. The first time a girl sucked my dick was at the age of 18. The last time was two years ago.

I tried to have sex with my last girlfriend, but all she did was punch my dick and get into this sadomasochistic, race-play game. ...We are not together at the moment.

It was these girls in the past that really influenced me to wake up to the bigger things I like.

I made my mistakes. Everyone has regrets. A regret is simply an honest choice, but rather, we tend to play an imaginary game and say, "if only I did this instead," which is not possible. No one can live out a perfect life with no mistakes in it.

Life is not a word processor where you can go back and edit the words you typed in.

So, everyone dreams too much of being a protagonist to an anime that no one is watching. Of course, the reality is, life is not an anime.

I remember in middle school that they would always tell us to line up and wait in the cold for a "hurricane drill emergency." As if a hurricane will come in a state where it never happens.

And then awkwardly, everyone stays outside and waits in the cold.

This time, from that same English class, I had a chance to stand right next to that ugly girl.

I first thought to myself, "What a drag! This is so annoying!"

I noticed that whenever these drills do happen, the other kids break up the line and start hanging out in their cliques.

Years later, they do the same exact thing in high school, and the same in an undergrad dorm as well.

I remember too, being outside, at 2AM in the dark cold, in a major city, while all these early 20s, baby college kids acted like everything was in middle school again. It is really a sad event to experience.

My brother once told me that the problem with white people today is that they are "white niggers." Yes, totally dependent beings that have no aim in life, but let the institution write their lives for them. We live off Mom and Dad's trust fund, and we use our money to spend it on decadent things. Once the money is gone, you're back at your parents' house. ...At least you're saving money if you are living at home.

You could say I lived in a neighborhood full of rich, white-nigger kids.

I didn't make friends in middle or high school. I was a shadow that haunted other students, looking for other "friends" that liked KMFDM too (It was impossible, especially if your other favorite band is Whitehouse).

In reality, I was the only "special snowflake" in my conservative school. And I take that with pride! Since the term, "snowflake" today could also mean, "rich-white-nigger-anime-kid."

I didn't know how to start a conversation. I did things when I was commanded to do them. I was looking for God to put me in a situation where I could be myself.

I think it happened at that moment.

I remember just standing in the cold and that ugly girl with the black hair was holding herself, like she had no jacket on.

She looked backed at me.

She always looked angry and mean.

And she said, "Joe, let me borrow your jacket. It's so cold out, I could die out here!"

I was nervous when she said. Not that I liked her, but because I had paranoia and anxiety, if I was to do something wrong, I would forever be hated by her.

I remember being anxious and saying, "Umm, okay, hold on, let me..."

...I was super feminine when I was 14. I remember seeing my first concert at that time in April. Les Claypool.

...And the first time I rubbed my dick on my bed and ejaculated to the thought of a cute Asian girl!

Things were going on in my life I could not explain. I felt like I needed to be a good person in order to fight the trauma I was going through.

You could say I was the perfect little Asian kid. Just not Asian.

I gave her the jacket to wear. And she put it on.

The best part was, she didn't thank me. She looked the other way while I stood behind her. The awkwardness began. Even though I was never conscious of an emotion called "being awkward," I never felt it. But I think she did.

We were quiet for three more minutes. She stole my jacket as if I was never there.

I know what you're thinking. "This girl is Chinese and she was using her Chinese shaming skills and ripping you off by feeding into your pathological altruism."

This is what I hear from most white guys today. I don't know why they think like this. Maybe they all "grew up" and they gave up on the beauty of Asian girls. ...But that's another story.

All the kids back then would scream and yell at each other and we would wait outside until we were in pain about it.

I would stand there, looking at everyone, and thinking to myself, "Are they good friends? They must be good." Again, I thought I would magically be bumped into someone nice.

The gook girl looked at me again. This time, she said something peculiar.

"What are you doing? Give me some space. ...Don't be doing something crazy like you always do Joe."

Then another girl showed up next to her. She wasn't talking to her or anything. She did say hi to her. Only then, did she have to look back at me again and say something.

This time, it was important.

"Joe, who are you going out with for the dance?"

...The Dance? I didn't even know there was such a thing coming up. The only variation of a dance to me is called a "prom."

She said it to me like she had to complete a sentence while balancing the discussion with her girlfriend. She was never talking to her and was using this as a way to start up a conversation.

"Who are you going out with? You're probably going to choose someone so unlike yourself and make such a scene on the entire night."

As she said this, she was trying to make her other girlfriend laugh as well, like if it was some kind of joke at me.

I remember looking down on the ground and being embarrassed at such a comment. I would pretend I wouldn't hear what she said. I made a smirk or a chuckle to make her quiet. I didn't like to talk to people back then. I thought having a conversation with her would only lead me to be hurt again. I had enough emotional damage at home from a verbally abusive father and an overprotective mother. I thought the same would happen if I approached my peers.

"What? You're not going to say who you're going out with?" I remember her saying. Her full-on, "tiger mom" was coming out.

I didn't want to say anything else. I remember saying, "I don't know," while looking down on the ground.

The bell rang and finally everyone had to get inside again.

She was saying something else too. I can't remember.

As we walked in, she stood right next to me walking. I think she was trying to reach for my hand. Though I was still hesitant.

This time, my feelings were growing towards her.

She had my jacket on still. And this time, she looked like a bossy person with a warm heart. I thought about asking her out for a date.

And then these strange thoughts started to enter. I was rethinking everything I knew about her and how I looked at her.

She said to me as we headed indoors, "You have a week to decide who you want to be with. Don't you know who you're going out with?"

This time she looked at me with her eyes. They were slanted, yes, and you might say ugly looking. I thought the same thing about another Chinese girl named Sophie. I thought to myself, "Why is Sophie even in this country when she doesn't even speak English, and she looks like some kind of pillbug?" I remember having those first thoughts about Asian girls. But this girl, I was in line with, was a part of the slow influence that would change my entire perception about them.

She had such an ugly, evil, and mean face. But this girl, when she looked at you, was begging you to do something important. She wanted me to uphold a certain responsibility or was trying to tell me something about myself.

That head of hers, like a football. And her dried black hair. Her eyebrows that go down slanted like somebody etched it into her faces. Her eyes are like an insect's. I remember she had some pimples on her chin too.

Even though I had enough of her "bullying" me, I said something like...

"Why would I want to go to the dance anyway? All the popular kids go and they are all stupid!"

She laughed at me,

"What? Are you crazy? That means you're stupid too if you go!"

I saw her smile for the first time. And she was smiling at me. I realized how white her teeth were. How her teeth contracted with everything so ugly about her. I love teeth by the way.

I have some racist friends who will talk to me how dumb and ugly black people are. About how black people have big lips, nappy hair, monkey like features, all that stuff. I can agree with what they mean by that.

...but to put that logic, any Asian girl, in *that* category, is unjust. Asians are the opposite of Black people.

Me and that girl both went to the same class. I forgot what else we were talking about. But we both had to go to the next class. She always said "goodbye" to me.

"Bye Joe," as she waved her hand.

Something was up. I knew she wanted to go to the dance with me. But I never did ask her out for the dance. I did something else with my family that week.

I remember graduation. She would approach me and try to have a conversation. I didn't know how to be social. I didn't get what she was saying. I knew there were open windows to create that friendship. But no one ever told me how to make friends.

Long story short, this girl liked me. Later, I realized how much I liked her too. I never had the words to express it.

…Years later, during my Junior year of undergrad, I had a Chinese girlfriend by the name of Chloe. Every Chinese girlfriend I had always had an American version of their Chinese name. Chloe was one of them.

I remember hanging out at her dorm. This was two years ago. We were really close and we did a lot of fun stuff together. I met her at the dance club while both of us did Tango. Something about dancing really speeds up an intimate relationship between two people.

We were on the couch together watching *The Big Bang Theory*. I don't even like that show. I insisted we watch basketball instead.

First, it starts off watching TV and you sit right next to each other. Then she moves in and cuddles right next to you. Within 30 minutes, footsies and handsies start to take action. And then, like cuddling in bed, both of us get horny and we start to make consenting clues what we really wanted from each other.

After two boring sitcom episodes, I told her I was horny in a quiet whisper. She was too. I was feeling myself.

She had in mind a blowjob.

She threw off the blankets, pulled down my pajama shorts, and started to lick and kiss my dick.

I'd shaved a few nights ago, so no pubic hairs would get in her mouth.

She was a slow sucker. A cute one too. Typically, she closed her eyes and used both of her hands. She slobs on it too like an animal.

I loved looking at her black hair and her football face while she put my entire thing in her mouth without a complaint.

She would then spit the whole thing out, laugh and say, "This is so awkward!"

She loved it.

And she would continue back at it giving me a soft salvia massage.

I couldn't take control myself sometimes and would say, "Do you like my cock?'

She would knob her head while sucking.

And then she would blurt out, laughing, "I like that white devil cock!"

I found that very humorous.

I admit, we would both get into "race play." Even we both didn't know what that was. I liked to call her math teacher, or tiger mom, or bug girl.

I think I might have said, "You look like a praying mantis."

And she said back, "I should rip off your head for saying that!"

And it was those white teeth she had. Such an ugly, gook-looking face you might call her, but her white teeth made her so human.

...And that's what made me think of that girl called Stephanie when I was in middle school. The same girl that was mean to me, wore my jacket, and tried to ask me out to the dance in a strange way.

Chloe was that girl again. Reborn. She was sucking my dick this time.

My one friend told me there is such a thing called "chaos magick." That if used correctly, your sinful dreams can come true. In the past four years, I started to exclusively masturbate to the Asian girls that I like. And now, I earned a girl that I desire and want to be with. That image in your head, over and over again, becomes a reality. Realize the dream, and it will become true.

...That girl in middle school will forever haunt me.

***

...It seems like watching porn with Asian girls in it is better than reality. I'm not kidding or joking. Go ahead and search in the Xvideos bar, "thai girl bar," "chinese college blowjob," "filipina sex," etc. ...The women look like better people! Maybe that's what I should do. I should use some sketchy call-girl service, and get laid by a 40-year-old Asian mom no one wants. Am I a loser for making that preference? Already sex stuff has happened to me in the past. I would have nothing to lose if I was to go about it with that. I mean, I would rather lift weights, sweat and lose calories, till my little stomach goes back into my body, and then I can approach some Asian hooker with the upmost confidence. Already, I have this advantage because I am young. That's not stopping me. The problem is, using the powers I have now, at this very moment.

This is the problem living in the middle of nowhere. No power means being in jail. I would have to get up, go somewhere, and do business over there. Then somehow, I would make it back to my parents' house. If I lived in the city, I would have easy access to these things. I would not have to worry. Living out here on my own, power shrivels up and dies. It's why most morons become Christian, realizing living out here, in the middle of nowhere, leads to suicide and nihilistic pondering. However, I can deal with it. Most people can't. People who have to deal with it too much grow up and get autism. Like all my oppressed friends. ...I don't have autism. I am abused by this doldrum system.

Ironically, this is what white people like to cry and bitch about in *Stuff White People Like*. Eventually, all the "right kind of white people," move out and live in New York or Los Angeles while "the wrong kind of white people," must suffer living out in nowhere. Not that I am striving to be "the right kind of white people," it's that I will have to live

113

out the consequence of not having access to the right things. Which ironically, in the natural event of things, I SHOULD be getting.

We live in such a competitive world. To imagine it was so different 70 years ago. Even 1000 years ago!

What's wrong with our country? Is America about living in a prison sentence while doing decadent things?

Where am I supposed to go find cute Asian girls? Is it a supply and demand ration thing and a fad of our generation?

The life of porn has it better. I am not talking about professional "porn actresses" (maybe I am) and the culture they have, I am talking about anybody with a camera, and having the guts to upload sex on the internet. ...So, people like me can view it.

I have been saying this since I was 21. But, when will someone watch pornography without jerking off? Is that even possible? Is art better when you... jerk off? I always had to consider porn being a... cultural anthropology.... some kind of altruism... about the subject having sex.

Like Holden Caulfield and his hooker... I want to know more about you. Why bother?

People are afraid to ask those big questions. In fact, a liberal watching porn, or just about anyone, will say, "she has a terrible life and you don't even know it!" Why should that be true, when in some autistic way of life, she is doing what she loves. She is human after all. And she could be a better human than the boring Asian girlfriend you're dating right now! To note, that she is getting a big, white, juicy cock to celebrate. That she is telling all her other Asian friends (who will watch her videos) that she is in a power-discourse, and she is the center of it. Porn videos are a list of her accomplishments. She proves she is a beautiful woman. This is her life and destiny. And she's a goddess for having this power. People will disrespect her power. But this is who she is, and all the men that will have sex with her, will be telling stories of her accomplishments.

Something Cicero said... about how the strong men lead lives of experience and accomplishments.... when the weak man... stays at home... and writes the accomplishments. It is advised that the strong man should write down his activities. But because of his on-going activities, he fails to write anything down, or even learns how to write. Ironically, the weak man, that failed to be the strong man, writes daily events down... records history. I guess that would be me. I am jealous that this life was not meant to be that of a Porn actor hunting down beautiful Asian women (to meet, to talk, to have fun, to love).

I can only watch things far away and contemplate on my life.

And they say to the weak mean... "be strong!"

It's not possible. My destiny has its own folds. The liberal tries and gives strength to people they wish, simply because they want it to happen that way.

Who cares about other people? When having sex with Asian girls twice a week is a priority? Nothing to complain there!

FUCK YEAH DUDE!

The fucking pussies at my little bitch college got fucking BUTTHURT over TRUMP'S VICTORY.

HOLY FUCKING SHIT DUDE.

lmmmmfaaaooooo.

This is going to be one fucked-up last semester. Haha. All these little bitch feminists and their blue lips… they won't be logging into Snapchat or checking their fucking Tinder anytime soon. Bitches having their period. Daddy Trump has got the stuff.

Haha. Best part of the day was hugging this cute black girl… she got SOOO fuckin triggered! Man, I got to feel her titties too. And act like I could also ask her on a date later. Too close! I got to hug TWO black girls in the same day. They looked up to me and are like "Dave, you're so sweet, please, please, please, fuck me when you have the chance!" lmaoo gonna get some of that later.

Soooo many bitches triggered in one single day. And it's fucking raining too. Such a sad, sad, day for these uptight bitches. Holy shit, I've been there for Trump since that March date in West Chester. Man, all my bros were there n shit. Sooo fun to get drunk and yell TRUMP TRUMP TRUMP TRUMP. Hellll yeah.

Was hitting iron an hour ago. Trying to work on my upper-body. Gettin pumped like any UFC fighter. Pow-pow! Hitting the bag like no tomorrow. Keep hitting that shit.

Everyone at school… such a little bitch. I'm like the only guy here. I play soccer, but still… ALL THE GUYS ARE

ON THE SOCCER TEAM. Dude, it's funny no-pussy land. All the girls are like virgins and don't know how to fucking party.

The only girls I like are the Asian girls.

It's not like I have yellow fever or anything, it's just that... dude, holy shit. THICK ass, CURVY body, SLANT eye... Ha, not that I'm racist or anything... but it's damn fucking cool to get with one.

First semester... got with this one. Her father was white (she looked white to me). And she definitely had that bossy Tiger mom attitude about her.

Well, it was like... "diversity day" or some gay shit. Really G rated stuff. Told her, "yo want a beer." Got with a bunch of friends, hanging out beside the library (no one saw us), just cursing and giving a shit about this.

And then she asked me to go to her dorm.

Booty-call!

It's not like I met her on the spot. I knew her class. I was looking at her, she was eye-fucking me. You know, something was going on and I saw it. I mean like, she likes Drake. Who doesn't like Drake? Also, helping her out with homework, barely made it out. And then sending snaps on bogus nights. It goes from there...

But seriously, after the weed, it went from Netflix chill to 9 o'clock fucking.

Amazing. The. Ass. Is. Real!

Banging on her fucking bed like it was the cops on her. Not like it was rape or anything, but fffffucking good sex. Came on her ass... did it again on her hair. Hair... sexy black hair. After that... pretty much skipped that Friday school morning... Cuddle party for 8 hours. 8 hours dude! I'm not joking! This is real! The hype is real!

Asian girls! Fucking A+ better than bitchy virgin girls.

Yo, she likes me, and I like her. I mean, hopefully I can get out with my Criminal Justice degree... and she like is going to med school. Going to go down now. Buy a house... get that job, Verizon possibly, idk. But like, seriously, it's going down.

I'm going to wife this girl.

I got no one to talk to, but still, I think my friends know. Hell yeah, I met them yesterday at Hooters to talk about it. Fuck the Hooter girls dude, ALEXIS IS THE ONE. I LOVE YOU.

Man, not like I'm a pussy or anything. I know what this is about. Joe has been teasing about how I'm going to have Gook kids, dude, not if they play fucking football or listen to rap. Besides, Alexis is like... really she's like half Chinese. That's not like it fucking matters or anything.

I mean, I know some fucking nerds in high school that dated real Chinese girls. I still don't fucking like them. They couldn't even last in a fucking fight with me. I remember this one nerd, used to be in my science class.

Dude, he's got issues.

This fucking kid would not shave. Nope. Looked like the unibomber. And like, that gay ass Mega Man shirt he would wear, EVERY. FUCKING. DAY. And his voice. When he talked, he sounded like Steve Urkle, and he's not even black! He just sits in class... looks at his little gay iPhone, like he's deaf or something, and failed to use eye-contact. This kid probably was like retarded or something.

And yet, before and after class, dude... his girlfriend was fucking Chinese. This girl was fat, cut her hair like some kind of doll, and acted so robotic. She'd be on him hugging him like some gay Disney movie. And she's like fat and ugly looking, and this tall retarded kid, with a terrorist beard, needs a hug from this. Don't get me started, but they kiss and it's ugly. Ug-ly. Slobber all over the place. And she... that girl. She wraps her arms around her like it's his little king. Oh yeah. So great. And she doesn't move her head away from his. Makes me so angry. She really deserves better. And this goofy idiot.

Yeah, I just remembered his name.

Jack. Mother fucking Jack.

What a nerd. I burn with anger, envy when I hear that name. No offense to other Jacks, but this is the Jack of all trades. This Jack. The Jack that gets this bug like creature hovering over him like he's a king.

This bro don't even lift. Not one muscle on him.

I bet you in a fight I can tumble this faggot on the ground. Put me in a ring with him. He would pretend he would be a boxer, putting his gloves up in the air like a fake defense. And then POW. Punch him right in the face and he'd go down. Would street kick him from there.

These weak people, like Jack, they don't know half the story of life. Jack is living off a trust-fund mommy and daddy built up for him. He won't even work until he's 26. And what's he like now... 20? No experience in the world. He's looking to get free sex with that bug like creature? Pathetic. This dumbass, weak society really gives the weak the benefit in life. Not even for the hardworking people that really deserves it. My dad works the night shift from 11:30 PM to 10:00 AM. He only sleeps in the day and is the most fucked up person ever. Does he get a lot of money? Hell yeah. That's something every man is not willing to sacrifice.

Jack and his bitch, it's a phase. Hit him while he gets out of school with a shitty degree in "English," 23, and then his Asian bitch is back in Maryland, while he stays around Virginia. What's he supposed to do? "Hey, let's just be friends?"

Fucking weirdo. No different than a rapist.

I have priorities. Wake up every day for soccer practice. Normal shit. Tell the bros I don't give a fuck. Crack a few gay jokes. Real animal shit. Jack... gay fag watches anime and looks at his ceiling for 4 hours a day. And he takes pride getting A+ in his homework assignments, and yet the teacher is doing it on purpose to make EVERYBODY feel good (even the stupid niggas, haha).

The difference is clear. He lives in shitty Anderson hall, where he has to suffer between closet space and fucking late at night... Dude, at least I got fucking Mayflower, big dorms for big men. Party zone. Unlike Anderson... real nigga shit.

Jack is whack. I don't know what his problem is.

I met Alexis doing normal shit. He met his girl online. It's true! Or maybe they both suck so much they got no one to go to but themselves. And they private towards their loneliness. Sad. But true.

I should start giving Jack shit. No really. I should. It's my last semester. Who the fuck cares?

...Gotta do homework shit now.

(In your best French accent, read the following commentary):

"Ho! Ho! My-my! The stupid people and their safe-spaces! A word made up to insult this shitty world! These low life idiots! I am on my typewriter and will set a 60-second-wipe out against the entire world! The ass of an English teacher, tells me 'point-blank' on a subject he can't comprehend either. Or better yet, doesn't want to unravel its follies. My-my, the idiots we have to deal. I can smell my cat shit in the next room. What else do these buffoons want? Deleuze, the man who survived academia, only to use his own rhetoric and get out shit-tasted ideas! How radical! How supreme! What a genius! The pathetic discipline of 'English' as a whole. These bastards don't want to learn Japanese or math. Losers! They want to play word games! I will show them a word game, a word game that hits close to the truth! And then, the whole world will go on fire! Haha! Deconstruction is a fraud!"

(He starts hitting his typewriter with intentions on world domination. He writes the following):

…Why start a revolution if people are happy with what they got?

There isn't any proper reason to complain. Everyone has their own private world and no one cares about the bigger picture.

In fact, it is a liberal ethic to become more "aware" or "wiser."

Also, why start a revolution if nepotism is the center of the American economy?

The American Dream is dead not because of an unfair ruling system, but because it denies a certain reality of nature.

Your profession is determined by how many friends you have.

It's doesn't take a rocket science to know this.

Tell anyone this truth and they go berserk.

Why would the American system lie to anyone that it is only connections that makes a good life?

That means, public and higher education was a waste of time. Working a day job is a waste of time. Consuming other products has not benefit. And creating art and investing in hobbies in the most ultimate waste of time.

We've been lied to.

Why would they lie? Because our elites have a foundation in liberalism and the post-enlightenment.

"Education," comes before nepotism. Even though it is nepotism that is the basis of the Left trinity.

Friends, Family, Freedom.

Friends. Everyone has them. Some friends are serial killers, movie directors, and prostitutes. Expect to be like them.

Family justifies your existence. The family created the law the connection of strangers. Family is stable to a healthy, happy life. It is the family that gives us meaning.

Freedom is what we all dream of. If only we did not have to hunt and kill for food. If only we did not have to struggle to woo over a lover. If only we did not have to physically fight to get a point across. Freedom means to do what we desire. Everyone has a different meaning of freedom. But all freedom can agree upon that is it law and the rules that stops freedom. Freedom allows people to become gods.

...ironically, some freedom harms other people's freedom (some animals are more equal than others).

America is based upon a private, liberal, free life. But freedom cannot be consumed alone. People need Friends and Family. It is family that gives people friends and freedom. It is friends that make family and freedom. Desire is the ultimate rule.

It turns out, only winners can obtain friends, family, freedom. The lower classes give them their own friends, family, and freedom. Everyone is in their own bubble minding their own business. That's American life.

My life is therefore justified. Accordingly, I don't have to do anything else! I already have the family to back me up, some useless friends that have their own perversion, and the freedom of consuming. This is American life. I'm sure my friend Nate, his family all graduated from Ivy league schools. Nate's friends are Jewish liberals, and the freedom he/she has is being a dickgirl. This trinity can only be afforded by the higher classes. I have to do what's best and aim for middle-class things.

Life is utterly boring.

Revolution is needed because this life is not natural. Animals are free every day. We have to "work" for our freedoms. But the truth is, no one really works to get anything. Everyone fucks their friends and find their faith. We are more animal than we deny being.

Revolution is needed because we are not honest. We lie to get ahead. We get caught up in our own intellectual language and confuse the normal human. Liberals corrupt humans into liberals. If we were honest, we would have a system that caters to our own family's interest. Strangers run the system.

And revolution is needed because there are too many people, too much mass- production, too much technology, and destruction of the earth. The Western World is consuming the earth until it has lived each 90 years of life completely. No one gives a damn after death. The religion is hedonist nihilism. No one cares anymore.

There is also a wrong type or Revolution. I am not a leftist or liberal. A "revolution" is often fantasized by the left. They want to "liberate" barbarians into liberals. They want everyone to speak their own rhetoric. This life is boring and inhumane. They are Buddhists trying to break out of the wheel of reincarnation. A revolution cannot have agitation. A revolution is natural, just like the four seasons. A revolution is religious.

The left is the true poison of humanity. It infected the West and now the rest.

When will the left realize their agenda is nothing more than the intellectual interest of Pan-European people worldwide?

There needs to be a nationalist revolution. A natural revolution from the so-called "right." This is not a proper term. Otherwise, the left must recreate itself and learn of its error.

I propose an "alt-left."

A left that denies The French revolution, Communism, and The Frankfurt school and after.

It will be based on a better obtainment of friends, family and freedom. It will be a racially aware left. No equality or universalism!

And no nepotism! Everyone is your friend according to your family! See the left/right broken logic there? Blasphemous.

Good fences make good neighbors.

No strangers will try and dictate my life.

I am an ordinary person that fears god. I want to live like an animal. No liberals will put me in a zoo. They are denying the jungle they belong too.

That will start a revolution. And the end to private and perverted America life.

…Fuck High School and the religion it has created!

Mom tells the evil genius that dinner is ready. He stops his type ranting and gets off.

"...I never, ever sat down at Starbucks until now. I am quite the anti-social person and not in the whole normative sense of... well, socializing. This is an interesting place though, nonetheless, to write a blog piece. Which I really don't feel like writing. —Here we go again," Will writes.

Will was waiting at Starbucks for his girlfriend Angie.

"It's a busy place. Nice people, in their 30s, that teach elementary school. Really feeling like I don't belong here now."

Will would write self-aware commentary to himself and later upload it on his Tumblr if he had the chance. He doesn't have a huge following. Only his friends he knows about punk shows. Will thinks aloud by typing.

"I haven't seen Realicide in forever. Hopefully, I can catch this show in December. I have no one to go with. I don't think Angie would be interested in shirtless young teenagers. Sounds like a gay novel. But I have class. Why would I bring her to such an event, when I could bring her to Hibachi? They cook on the grill for you. I believe in a romantic dinner. I really don't like the idea of hanging out at bars. Deep inside, I want a traditional, loving, and beautiful relationship. That will follow, hopefully a year later if we are still around, and I get to... 'pop' the question. The classic, the nerdy, 'will you marry me?' I'm honest. And then I can plan the wedding at the Japanese house, and then we move into the city. I always hinted to her at this, but seriously, three kids! I'm an only child. Three kids are worth it. I can't have one child. It has to be three. I have the money stored away. I really can do what I want. This whole punk veneer is a joke. It's not me. It's a hobby that leads to boredom. I guess we can still have both things. You can be like Xiu Xiu, and I can like Cold

Cave… and then, we can be professionals. Day jobs. Asking, 'how are the kids?' Father and mother. I want that. I want to be an adult soon. 27, it's that feeling of isolation. I didn't go college. I barely made it out of high school. Angie is so lucky to go to med school. She's almost done. I don't want to be a bum and live off her money. I can get extra money with this Verizon job I have now. I can climb the ladder. Watch me become officer. I can stay in the office and boss people around. Go home, see how she is…"

Deep in meditation, there was Angie and her bike. She parked it aside. Looked right at him. She smiled and waved her hand up. Coming right in the store to sit right next to him.

"Hi Will! What are you doing here hanging out? This is so unlike you," she said.

Both laughed a bit. Will was anxious to talk to her. He folded his MacBook away.

"Well, it's actually about work. About how I am going to get a raise," he said.

"Really? Good job!"

"Thanks, I hope it works out."

"Don't worry! You're a great person!"

She smiles at him. Wide white teeth. The anxious feeling Will is feeling. Acknowledged. Turning the discussion around.

"So how was your week?" Will said.

"Good. Nothing much happened, had to go see Mom."

"How is mom?"

"Good! She is good! She is ok and doing fine."

"Tell her I miss her and she is a nice person too."

"Haha, I think she knows that."

"I mean, I would like to go out to dinner with your family again. We did it once, and I felt like, maybe we should do it again. But this time, I won't do anything that might... you know, shame the family?"

"Don't worry about it. Dad is a little mad about that, but it will all go away."

"Seriously, I didn't know. I am sorry too that I don't know any Chinese and that I didn't know anything before. You didn't tell me..."

"Relax Will. It's ok. It's good!"

She smiled again. Every time she smiles, Will's blood rushes. The first time he met her was two years ago at a punk rock party. And the very first time Will met Angie, he still felt he could not approach her. Two years later, and he hasn't accomplished being excited over Angie's smile. His heart. Throbbing. Hurting this time. An unheard voice. He needs to get closer. Closer this time. They had sex. It was good. Twice they had sex. And sex is a controversial issue with her. But the next time they do it, it's going to be the first kid. Will is going to have to calm down his emotions and speak his mind. It's going to be soon. Today? It might be right.

Happy together.

"That's good to hear. Um, what are you doing tonight?" Will said.

"I heard over Facebook Jeff is going to have party over his house tonight."

"Is that on 32nd street?"

"Yes, between 31st and Shell."

"Got it. Not like I'm going by myself tonight. I need to know these places."

"You know where I am. You know where my apartment is too. Jeff is only a block away."

"Yeah, I know. I don't want to get lost like always."

"When do you get lost? I don't recall you being blind."

Then the goofy conversations kick in. About jokes, about their personality types. Cracking on their flaws. The whole, "remember that one time," funny stuff. Maybe stuff about online jokes. Popular news. Bands. They like bands. Will and Angie tried to start a duo together. Him on drum, she's the screamer and guitar. It didn't go so well. They had practice sessions. Never got to play at a house party. It really was a tool to get Will and Angie closer. After a night of noise, they would go to bed, watch YouTube and cuddle. Cute stuff like that. One thing leads to the next. Bands are now like... dates. They are no longer music journalists and looking for fun. They look for fun together and tell how they feel about music.

Will has ADHD. Music is important to his life. He never was a musician. He was forced to play guitar at 15 and get his guitar lessons with it too. He failed at it. He got so resistant, that he would only now play the sitar and only wants a sitar teacher. He dropped that too when he hit 18.

Sometimes, a song would pop in Will's head at times when he's happy. Maybe this is common among people. After conversation, a break from it, no one talking to him, there is that one song that dominates the day and floats in his head.

While Angie went to go to the cashier to get lunch, Will could not stop thinking about that one song by... Depeche Mode. *Nothing's Impossible*. It was on *Playing the Angel*. His dad took him to go see Depeche Mode during that time. This is a time in the band's career where there is no Alan Wilder. This was rather a Depeche Mode sounding revival without Wilder. A post-modern Depeche Mode. That song, it sounds so... deadly.

Even the stars look brighter tonight
Nothing's impossible
I still believe in love at first sight
Nothing's impossible

It has that classic, evil Neo-folk sound to it, and is sinister. Every post-hardcore band would dream of making a song like this. It goes so well with the mood. It's romantic, but it's not pussy-like. It's a masculine way to address the situation. Even if he has to deal with Angie's teeth. The very teeth that once grind on his dick a year ago.

Sometimes, he can juggle the songs in his head. Another pop song he remembered when he was a little kid was a club song. He was into electronic dance music more than this punker stuff. He still is, but doesn't tell anyone. That song is by Satoshi Tomiie. Up In Flames. A cheesy dance song back then. Not too old. Will is an aficionado about club songs. His older brother was a Drum and Bass DJ.

Will knows his obscure gems. This is not the original Psy-
trance version. Will remembers the album mix.
Kelli Ali sings,

So, what kind of voodoo do you do?
What kind of voodoo do you do?
What kind of voodoo do you do to make me feel this way?

Up in flames
Up in flames
Up in flames
My love will go up in flames with you

That kind of song. It was a dance song for the English.
Amazing that a Japanese worked with Frankie Knuckles in
1989. If Ali stayed in Sneaker Pimps, everything would've
been fine. Still, her solo albums are pretty good. This
catchy song, avoiding everything and tuning back into
Angie. Songs like this pop in Will's head.

After an hour or so at Starbucks, it was time to walk out
down 28th. They would reminisce of the people they knew,
their first dates, about family, the good stuff. Eventually, at
the end of the block, Angie would have to ride her bike
back to campus.

"See you at Jeff's, right?"

"Yeah."

"Ok, see you then Will. Bye."

"I love you."

"I love you too."

They didn't kiss this time. He would see her later tonight. Will walks back to his place where he parked the car.

The city. One big cluster of upper-class yuppies, not knowing what they are doing in their lives.

Will didn't have much to do in 6 hours. Drove back home. Made himself pasta for dinner. Fed the cats. This guy lives alone. YouTube keeps him company. The stress about seeing Angie again. He never told her he was alone most of his time. The days when he's not called in for work. Every guy has to make an impression that he is busy and doesn't have time for silly games with girls. Will wants someone by his side. If anything has damaged Will's life most of all, it's his lack of self-confidence and abandonment issues. He will not drive to places if he hasn't been there before. He needs a friend to go with. To be a loner, a life he didn't deserve. And sometimes, what if Angie has a better social life than him? He stays away from Snapchat, knowing that it is a device of jealousy. This thing that tells the anti-social they are failures. Will is tired of making up a facade that he is a playboy. He's not. He's just some guy.

After doing nothing for a long time, after watching the sun go down in the city, when outside turned cold and the moon showed up, Will was ready to go. He'd taken a shower beforehand and wore his favorite designer shirt. The spreadshirt with the goofy Japanese patterns on it. Now to drive to the place.

He parked a few cars away. Will often gets his places confused. "I *think* this is Jeff's place. Am I *allowed* to go in?"

The red corner house with the brown door and a big Flyers sticker on it.

Knock at the door. And he also texted, "I'm here."

Jeff opened the door. "Hey! What's up? How ya doin?"

Shake of the hands and a hug. Will walks in the living room.

That strange living room. He's only been here once. This living room with the record collection, like a book shelf. Obscure hardcore bands. Nothing Will likes. And that old-style record player from who-knows when, to play those up-to-date punk records. Those records made this year on the singer's budget of $500. Not making a profit on them, but still. They exist.

The dirty table with the cigarette stains, the shitty hemp, the black, burnt whatever. Messy.

And when Will walked in the kitchen going forward. The small kitchen. The small kitchen with fridge opened. A cute Spuds Mackenzie sat atop of it. No reason. To the right, a big guy with his beer. Sitting on two crates, Chelsea and Angie.

"Hey," a soft whisper and wave from Will.

"Will!" an exciting cheer from Angie. A smile from Chelsea.

A hug.

They were back together again. A few chit chats and hello from people in the room.

"This is Dave. He's a nice guy," Angie said.

The big guy shook Will's hand.

"Sup homie," he said.

Tonight, there was a Flyers game. Jeff wasn't into that.
Dave was. He brought his girl along. She was good friends
with Angie. They met two months ago. Alexis was so
different from Angie. She was the type that… knows her
guys. Dave won her heart, for now.

Jeff was in the other room with Howie. Talking about
things. About the day and stuff. Jeff was high, most likely.
Will could talk to Jeff about music. But it wasn't until Jeff
would go on a tangent about his band he was trying to
form, Killmonger. Killmonger played some shows. It was
something to make Jeff feel good about. Will didn't get it.
Maybe because he liked electronic music more and could
care less and less, as the days go by, about hardcore. Jeff
would never leave it. Tattoos all over his left and right arm.
How could he get a professional job looking like that?

Howie was there for the weed and good times.

Will talked a bit to them. Only to get back to what he really
came for. Sentimental time with Angie.

"You ok?" Will asked Angie.

"Yeah, I'm fine, what's up?"

"Oh, nothing much."

This is how Will starts a conversation. It feels like it's about
nothing, until he leads it to something meaningful. And
then soon enough, the jokes start.

"Oh, my god. I can't stand that kid, Eric, with his long stupid hair! And like, I'm not sure if he has autism or not, but, he's so annoying. Like, does he care that I blog online about... racist stuff?" Will humorously addresses.

And Angie laughs along with Chelsea.

"Take it easy, it's not like he hates you or anything," Chelsea says.

"Well no, this kid is going to stalk me because I know what the hell the Alt-Right is!" Will replied.

A laugh from everyone. Jokes like that. About pain, prejudice, understandings. The things you can't say in the work space, but on the weekends, with trusted friends, you can. Cliche. But it works.

Then here they come! Matt, his girl Olivia, and Steven. Everyone shakes hands. All good time chats. Like a cute high-school reunion full of strangers. The party is growing. Will reserved a room upstairs before the party. He texted Jeff earlier about sleeping over. Enough space so he can sleep on one end, and the exciting part, Angie at the other end. If things go well.

The Flyers game begins. Dave and Alexis watching. Alexis was upstairs with her girl Karen. They are both smokers. They need a place to smoke outside near windows. Talk about dangerous girl stuff until Dave commands her so.

Karen is single. She is looking for that single guy. Howie is disgusting. Not him. Sooner or later, some cute boy will come over.

Will can't be too eccentric. He can be eccentric around Jeff. Maybe Steven. Will puts on his mannerly good face.

"Chelsea, where's Big P?" Will asks.

"Oh? Paul? He's got work! I know!" Chelsea explains.

Too bad Paul couldn't come over. Paul is a welder. Works at night too. A nice guy. Never went to college. Same with Will. Paul is more of a tough guy. That's something Will could not relate to.

Paul met Chelsea at a bar. Things went from there.

"The thing is, Paul is going to be with me this whole December. He's going to meet my family for the first time!" Chelsea said.

She looked at Will. Will was a little worried.

"What's wrong?" she said.

"Nothing. Reminds me of this one time..."

Angie butted in.

"Like the time you messed up around my family! I knew it!" Angie said.

A little nervous laugh from Will.

Paul is going to go through the same test Will had to go through. The dreaded and confusing Asian family.

"I think that's why you relate so well with Chelsea, Angie."

"Yep! I guess so!" she said.

All fun and games. Until mom and dad gets mad at you.

Where is Paul when you need him? The guy that makes the perfect comebacks in the right situation? That guy doesn't even speak Chinese. He's lucky enough to get an English speaking one, like it is some handicap to his personality. Chelsea is nice. Though, she is a pill popper. Good thing Angie stays away from drugs. Will never did drugs in his life, nor does he drink. Angie drinks. Only on occasions. That's the only time Will would drink too. With her.

Score for Flyers! Cries in the other room! Yeah! Screaming. Shocks Will for a bit.

The noise. How can you overcome such a tremor? It makes Will distant. Away.

Does Angie really like him? That's what he has been thinking about. Should he leave? This Dave, and Chelsea, and this Jeff and Matt, can't he get some peace? He has to act a certain way in front of them all. Like this stupid, know-it-all, white-person approved, socialite. Will doesn't want the attention or the action. He had the guts enough to see Angie today and to be with her. That, living alone, he can overcome his fear by channeling it through Angie. That is his award. Angie.

Does she care? Is it ok he is alone? He always made up a fib or two. Now like a war zone, like that stupid scene from *Saving Private Ryan*, where everything goes numb, is it time to *do* something with her? Will is actually anti-social. An introvert. This environment was not made for his survival. It's time to get out of the jungle.

"Angie, what are you doing?" Will said awkwardly.

"Uhh, nothing much. Just doing what everyone else is doing."

Will gets nothing out of that.

Karen walks down the stairs. She yells, "Oh my god, which one of you fuckers left a dirty ass condom on the bed? Clean it the fuck up!"

"Oh, shit man," Dave says while walking up the stairs.

Howie laughing. He looked like he was already out of it.

Steven came in to budge against Will. "Haha dude! Someone's getting fucked tonight!"

"Yeah," says Will, followed by a sarcastic "haha."

Angie and Chelsea laughing. Saying stupid stuff. That kind of stuff that would piss of Will. Isn't Angie Will's girl? Not stupid fucking Steven? Who the hell is he? Will had better act fast.

"Want to watch the game in other room?" Will says to Angie.

"Ok, sure," she says. She daintily gets up from her sitting, like a girl being asked to dance with her gentlemen. Will, grabbed her by the hand. And Chelsea who was sitting there watching, wishing Paul would come sit right next to her. Rather, that bastard Steven makes a move and takes Angie's spot.

"I thought you didn't like sport," Angie said.

"Well, um, you know, I was around it with my Dad, and we went to games together," Will said, making up a quick excuse.

TV was utterly boring these days. How can you watch the game? Fucking Eminem is blasting out of all things. Can't even hear the announcers of the game. Awkward. Letting Angie go through this is unethical. Why expose her to this? Howie had passed out now. Jeff, god knows what, smells like shit. Standing, watching the TV in a corner position.

"Nothing really is happening that much, let's go upstairs," Will says.

"Ok," she quickly said into submission.

Walking up the creaky stairs, Will has a silent thought to himself (remember how Garfield the cat thinks?)

"I hope this goes well. Hope I don't say something wrong. Hope I don't. This is it. This way. This way."

Luckily, an empty room is upstairs, past the room where Chelsea and her friend are smoking. Disgusting. "Punk" houses, as they like to call them, are disgusting. (SWPL culture is interesting when they start calling, yuppie, urbanite, collage-age living "punk.")

The room was a cozy one. Except the mattress was seated upon two concrete blocks. The window was covered with a large Taiwan flag. Knick-knacks on the floor. A broke bobble-head of Allen Iverson from the 90s. Not a romantic place. Will could make this place romantic. Now that Angie and him are alone. Shutting the door.

Angie sitting on the bed. Looking briefly at her phone. Texting? Hopefully her sister or her parents.

This was Will's chance now. He sits down right beside her.

"...A long day, yes?", Will didn't know what to say.
"Oh yeah!", a smile from her.

A loud noise comes roaring downstairs. The Flyers once again make a score.

"Angie, um, I was thinking. You know actually, it's going to take me two years until I get a BA in Communications? Right now, everything is good and I like working where I do now, but I am thinking about future plans."

"That's exciting Will! You should be so proud of yourself!"

"I know I am, I think. Like, I have a good job now, and, I think a degree would improve my income and..."

"It will!"

"It what?"

"You will get one, Will!"

Will is getting anxious. He forgot his own chain of thought.

She had a nice smile on her. No. This isn't another make-out session. Even though he could seize the moment and lay her down. She knew it too and would consent to it. That's how much they liked each other. Her eyes, so adorable. But no, he didn't bring her in here to fuck her. No. This is about love.

"Um, Angie, what are your plans in the future? You know, like next year?"

"What's that?"

"Um, I mean, like, you know. What are going to do after med school?"

"Haha, I don't know. Be a pharmacist? Why do you ask?"

"Well, I'm going to get a really good paying job too and... and..."

"YEEEAAAAAAHHHHHHHHH!!!"

Followed by loud "woos" and clapping. Obviously, something to do with the Flyers.

Will stopped for a second to hear them.

Angie looked at Will waiting for him to continue what he was saying. Will actually forgot what he was even trying to say in the first place.

"Well... I like you Angie," he smiled.

Angie smiled back, "I like you too Will."

Everything was going good. Will felt happy to express himself like that.

And his thoughts returned to him about what he was finally going to say to her.

"Angie, would you be interested in moving into this new place with me? It's real close by where you are and I plan on finishing college too."

Before she could reply, he added more to his statement like a disclaimer.

"I mean, I have money and some from the trust. It's enough to support you and you don't have to worry or anything like this is a contract..."

She was surprised.

"Oh really? Moving in? Why is that? Don't you see me enough in the day?" she smiled.

Will had to say something cunning.

"Not enough! I like seeing you every day and need you beside me like a parent!"

And he continued,

"And not like I am a little kid or anything. I want to be a responsible adult and I have a promising future. I want you to be by my side and we can progress together! ...like, really good friends!"

Angie liked what he was saying.

"Really? That's awesome! My place is boring with my other girlfriends. I'm just comfortable with what I have right now. But it's a nice thought to have."

"No! No! No! I really do mean it! I would like to stay with you and it's so boring when I am alone. I always feel like a loner and I am so much happier to see you every day! I have so much more meaning to get up every day and do something! You know?"

Amy thought about it for a second. Will actually was quite serious about this.

"Oh, well, where is this place at?"

"52nd Avenue. So close to where you work out. This can totally work out! We can move in only a day!"

"Really?"

"Yeah!"

"It's not a bad neighborhood, is it?"

"No! No black people in sight!"

"Haha, I believe you. And the grocery mart and..."

"Same as always. We can do this Angie and..."

A knock on the door, a girl peeked through.

"Angie-Angie! Ginny is here!" she said like an announcer!

"Oh great! Here I come!" Angie said.

She looked back at Will.

"I will be right back! Hold on."

Angie left the room as Will sat on the bed.

That awkward moment where now Will was alone in the room by himself. ...He said it. Now it's a matter of whether she will accept it or not.

Strange. He could have made out with Angie if he wanted to, but he had bigger plans. This wasn't about frivolous sex anymore.

Alone he felt worse. He could text someone right now or check out his social media. Read something online. And that's exactly what he did while he was waiting for her.

That utter feeling like he didn't belong to this bro-hang out party. Or whatever it was. A SWPL party. Angie could understand where he was coming from.

The strangest part of it all was that his Ginny is Asian too.

"...a bunch of white guys with their Asian girlfriends and pretending life is a party," Will thought to himself.

"I kind of like that."

The thought that this culture he was a part of was more than a phase or a lifestyle. It seemed like it was a genuine thing in life. Something rather of his identity.

He could hear Angie deep in girl gossip talk with Ginny. He decided to head out of the room and go downstairs to hang out the scene.
Will had terrible social skills. Why bother anyway?

A few hours later and some chit-chatting here and there, Angie and Will were outside the house talking again.

Whenever it was night in the city, everything got so cold.

When girls talk, they talk about silly stuff. "DJ Diamond Cuts," or something off topic. Will was never into every little thing Angie said to her other bird-like girls.

After getting down the important issues, Will had to remind her again.

"Angie. Think about it. Everything is under control and you're such a great person..."

Something cheesy like that.

"I will consider it Will. I always miss you."

She kissed him on the cheek.

"Bye Will! see you tomorrow!" She waved.

"Bye!" He did the same.

Alone yet again. Going back home slowly.

Alone again in his bedroom, going to bed.

Anxiety about tomorrow and the future.

...If only he would have changed his mind and had sex with her, and, maybe slept over. And then proposed to her about the house plan!

Things would've been different. Thinking deeply to himself.

He went too soft that time. Next time, go Alpha.

Who cares?

She said she would think about it. It will all happen.

...hopefully.

…Another day in small town Connecticut. Officer Cormack gets up in the morning. Right by his side is his wife, Alice.

A good morning kiss.

He brushes his teeth, gets on his own clothes, has his coffee, and fruit for breakfast.

He kisses his wife goodbye. "See you tonight. I love you." Another kiss.

Cormack drives to work.

The daily business, the boss, the usual officers, the afternoon routine.

Signing off. Cormack begins work in his cop car.

Just like this for five days of the week.

He will sometimes text his wife on duty. He will text his son or daughter's number from time to time.

What happens in the average day?

Many things. Sometimes, it's a guy busting a red light.

But the best part in the day is when there is a car chase. Cormack has had his fair trade of chases.

This one time, he drove on someone's lawn trying to catch one maniac. Got him. Caught him over the fence. Yelled at him. A traumatic experience. But Cormack gets high on that stuff.

When he was a teenager, he had to go to college for English. He hated it. Nothing to do. Boring. Alone. He is a different person than when he was a teenager. After his graduation, he put down that Nietzsche and Derrida, and joined a Brazilian jiu-jitsu club. No job. It was for fun.

And then the job fair came about, and he heard about the lucrative position of being a mall-cop. He joined the police academy right away.

A better experience than college ever was. He met masculine friends, got bigger, learned how to travel, and improved his social status. He was always an antisocial person. He is a more stoic person now.

And the best decision he ever made in his life… is when he joined Church on Sunday. He had no one, until he met her.

His Filipina wife.

She speaks good English. And she was looking for him. She never was promiscuous. She was afraid of White Americans. She thought she would never be good looking in front of one. Until they married two years later. She became a Cormack too.

They put both their money together and bought a house in a small town, a few miles off where Cormack originally lived.

He patrolled his own territory. He had his own family. He has his own thrills.

What changed it all?

When he read Yukio Mishima. He kept it a secret. He couldn't tell anyone. Sooner or later, he became a fan of Mike Cernovich, Jack Donovan. …The rest is history.

Cormack doesn't believe in White Nationalism though. He likes the idea of it. He cares more about his family. His older brother, his younger sister, his parents. They have their obligations.

Why didn't he know about this stuff when he was 18?

And before that? He would stay inside all day and play video games. He likes anime too, and still does. He may be goofy, but hardworking. He can't tell anyone at work he likes that stuff.

He doesn't like being a "bro" either. Nope.

Lifting weights cured his anxiety.

All he ever wanted was a beautiful girlfriend and an exciting life.

He's got one now.

The kids are entering middle school, and his wife still gives him amazing sex.

And when he goes to work, he could die. He could get shot by some stupid fucking nigger. Maybe he can shoot one back. ...And be on the hit list for Black Lives Matter.

Not gonna happen. Never happened. He pushed down many niggers before. Got away with the abuse too.

A true warrior.

Is this the life he is living in? A socratic world that pretends it's all but socratic, when the truth is, it's actually pre-socratic? The socratic people who deny this pre-socratic world. To win, one must be pre-socratic, not socratic.

That's the biggest lie today. Why do so many white people hate the cops?

…The day is about over. The sun goes down.

Officer Cormack calls it quits for today. He will do night service this Friday.

Comes home at 8. Kisses Alice. Eats. Checks on the kids. The kids love him. Showers. Back to bed. Watches the news. The simple bed talk before the lights go out. An hour or two later, "goodnight my love," and the lights go off. If things get really exciting, dry humping and kisses. "Not now, honey," she might say. Or the classic, "I got a headache."

And so, ends another exciting day with Cormack.

…If only.

If only he had the time to write down the life he has been through.

And, to finally be rewarded with this amazing existence! The existence he dreamed of since he was a bully in high school!

Physically and verbally abused. He survived it. That fake institution that lied to him about the world.

Still, he loves his job.

One day, when he retires, he should finally learn how to write properly, and write about his life. Or about how he saw things. He can't really do it. He barely made it out of that private college many years ago. The money spent on that too.

A happy life. But a sad, sad story that he cannot share his life with everyone else in this world.

He is doing amazing things. He doesn't need to write anything down about. Deep down inside, he wishes he could write about it.

This amazing life. This new identity. How can he?

When he wakes up, a new day begins.

The feeling of being happy every day is a rare thing.

AMA with Japan-based Alt-righter, Colin Liddell.

ANON: *What do you think of the Trump victory? What does it mean for the US and what does it mean for Europe? What do the people in Japan think about it?*

CL: The Japanese hate and fear Trump. They tend to take Trumpion hyperbole at face value, and swallow US MSM narratives with just a dash of soy sauce. Also, almost no-one here except me and Random Yoko (https://www.youtube.com/user/randomyoko2) thought Trump would win. They are in shock. This is good because it will make them more friendly to Mr. Putin when he comes here next month.

My take on Trump is not fixed. One ironic thing is that he is actually America's first post-racial president (not Obama who was a racist so-and-so).

Trump's "racism" is essentially that of the pragmatic businessman who wants the best people for the job and realises that America will only vote GOP if it stops going the way of California.

To reverse rather than just slow down the negative demographic trends, however, would require a LOT of unpleasantness that would play badly in what is still soft country with a liberal/leftist media and SJW college kid class, egged on by big business interests.

60-40 I think Hillary's victory would have been better for us...

PILLEATER: *You have been to Japan and taught Japanese (correct?). I think it's really interesting in the Alt-right that there is an "Asian-love" or "Japanophile" nature* *to it. I was an Asian Studies major and might consider it for a MA. My Japanese is Ok. I think I read somewhere that you did a review, or had an interest in Trevor Brown's art? He does remind me of the extreme, sadist, avant-garde art of Mishima and noiseband Whitehouse. Some Alt-right themes in there.*

Now, to the point of the question, what do you think about "the Asian question" in the alt-right? Meaning, what do you think about white-male Asian-female pairings and how these white males are straight up WN, alt-righters, or eccentrics? They can't just go back to their blue-haired fems and respect that in the white ethnostate. Where are they to go? Is it ok to have anime girlfriends that are real? And speak Japanese too? -Pilleater

CL: I hung out with Trevor Brown a couple of times. His art is cool but essentially degenerate. As for the Asian question, I think it's actually a bit cruel to create mixed race kids. They often seem to suffer toxic identity issues. But, yes, White women, raise your game - cats and purple armpits are no substitute for a nice White man, even if he does belch and fart a bit.

ANON: *I wonder if much of this is just due to random chance? I grew up with Japanese video games and cartoons, so I'm addicted to the stuff for life and wouldn't have it any other way. The fact that Japan provides a good model for a racially homogeneous nation is just an added bonus. And of course, a lot of people came to the alt right through 4chan, which started its life as an anime forum.*

EDIT: Although there's also an anti-Japan element to the online left, like with how they frequently criticize anime and manga for being sexist. So, there is something interesting

going on there, in terms of the personality types and the political interests that are attracted to the right and the left.

ANON: *What are your views on white men marrying Asian women?*

CL: Asian women have been unwittingly evolved to hack our White male sense of sexual attraction, but try to remember that much of this attractiveness is due to four factors - their neoteny, androgyny, thicker face fat, and more traditional upbringing. If you are attracted to Asian women, you are essentially attracted to childlike boyish women with chubby faces, who love their daddy. If one's infatuation with Oriental women goes beyond a certain point, you are likely to create people with rather toxic identity issues. Short version: handle with caution.

PILLEATER: *Interesting. I really liked that "neoteny" article of yours back on the classic alt-right website. The "childlike boy" part brings to mind a story by Mishima, "Omi." A high school story about gay love, found in Confessions of a Mask. Yes, that "toxic" thing needs to be addressed. It will create this Mishima complex too. ... Asian-Aryanism?*

I think it's really interesting in the Alt-right that there is an "Asian-love" or "Japanophile" nature to it.

This is one is called, "Easy Tiger." Dedicated to Harriet Sugarcookie.

She came in the room.

The camera filming.

Black, bowl cut hair.

5 ft something.

Really average compared to others.

An appetite that suppressed her consciousness.

She keeps this a secret from her family.

Now she's alone.

Abandoned.

Cute little bee hair-clips.

The little red bowtie.

Her Pippi Longstocking dress.

Those big, black glasses.

Her tits, not that good.

Sagging.

She's 28.

Works for a laundromat.

Nothing much to do in Bristol.

Good thing she met him at that bar.

The performer: Taller, built, handsome.

At least he lifts weights.

He didn't go to school either.

Works for the toll booths.

Charming personality,

With one slight defect.

He's hungry too.

Video, after video, after video.

A hobbyist for PornHub.

She, being his main star.

She, could care less.

She, liking everything on film.

She, could be his wife.

Her cute English accent.

Her fat boy-like face.

Her submissive personality.

Her whitewashed personality.

But body somewhere else.

Both consented to this?

I don't know.

Too hard to tell.

They might be acting on trauma.

Closing her eyes, as she sucks his uncircumcised penis.

How she happily likes to take the skin and suck the forehead.

Like a little turtle from its shell.

She's too happy about it.

Like this is her husband.

Up and down her head goes, against his stomach.

Like sucking something from inside him.

A mosquito.

An Asian mosquito.

Korean? Chinese? Not sure.

Not Japanese.

Her cute little picnic plaid shirt.

"I need you to fuck me," she lovingly says.

All on film.

Giggles.

There is something more to this.

Lifting that skirt, looking at her pussy.

And official sex that's quite good.

She looks like a doll.

Opening mouth, laughing, smiling, happy.

Like she might say any second, "I love you."

She has before.

No cum on her.

She tends to swallow.

Or gets it on the leg.

Like foreplay.

Very conservative.

This is what he does to her.

Different costumes, different movie, different acting.

So-called they are swingers.

Too hard to tell if they love each other.

Video after video, recapturing her rape.

Still, she is the same lovable person.

That type of Asian girl,

You wouldn't think she's like that.

But she is.

Any Asian girl, that you're in the same room with it.

That girl that likes anime.

And wants to be white instead.

The ugly one.

It could be her.

The fun she has, behind biology exams.

It could be you filming her.

It could be your lover forever.

It could be the life you always wanted to live.

Perpetual infinity.

The girl that's made for you.

...Pink room, Christmas lights, waterbeds, slow motion.

Andros felt all these things at once.

Laying like he was a crucified Jesus. A bed full of Tetra fish. All different colors, swimming as a rainbow school. Flashing up and down.

Andros, tired and beat from playing too much damn Dragon Quest 30. This newest game in the installment featured virtual reality. The first time ever in the series you could roleplay as a Fantasy version of an Akira Toriyama character. Yes, Slime is still in the game. And a sexy Slime girl too which is popular among female players.

Andros was in reality. Jacked out of the system. Inside, he was in "Dr. Maddox Call Service." His favorite place.

In the future, masturbation is obsolete. The theories of Dr. Alfred Kinsey have become a principle to this society. Sex is practiced at the age of 16. That is the legal age to enter a brothel. Don't think brothel like it's some disgusting place in the city. Brothels are now natural, like taking a daily shower.

Andros had on his favorite "Fiji cigarette" pink sweatshirt. You see, pink is Miyuki's favorite color. He wants to impress her tonight. Andros had been seeing Miyuki since he was 17. Everyone is assigned a call girl until they are married. Either they find someone or write to the Samsoft corporation that they want her. It is still controversial to have a call girl as a wife. Still stigmatized. There are social justice types that will say "they are people too." The same old story. Does he really like her?

161

The room is designed for each customer. So is the girl. Miyuki was made for Andros. If ever he marries, Miyuki is recycled and her past memories deleted. Call girls don't die until they are set free to marry. Then they are given the privilege to be human, not android.

The best part about call girls is that you never know who you're gonna get. There has never been a complaint about them. Since the age of 5, cat scanners phish out memory content, and corporations, like Samsoft, use this information to create the perfect mate. All call girls come from Asian genes. It has since become tradition. White people already have a white ethnostate out on some moon light years away. Terra (once called Earth) is the metropolitan planet no one wants to be on anymore. All the problems in the world have been solved. Got one? Go to a new planet. You see where this is going. If you don't have the credits, you have to stay home and surf virtual reality. Humans are no longer capital. They are the consumers.

Andros is a middle-class American. Attended public education, state school, and has a "reputation" in indirect sales. Degrees, such as the B.A. and PhD, are long gone of the past. It's all about getting famous on the internet and how much "post" users have. Andros can't compete. Too much anxiety. He wants to see the world. Just, how the heck is he supposed to have the creds to begin with? Life is good anyway!

Closing his eyes and opening them. Thinking. Looking at that ceiling. Andros has something on his mind. The room is pink. Pink is a color that soothes Miyuki and Andros. Rooms are never meant to cause pain. He is in… what you old people would call… a "safe-space."

"Yeah. I believe in myself. Nothing is wrong. Everything is ok. Life is a silver platter. If Donald Trump could do it, I can too!"

Andros lost in deep thought. Thinking about funny things. Was it worth playing Dragon Quest this afternoon? He's got to go back to work on Monday. Saturday is his only day off.

Classical music makes Andros feel ok about himself. He likes, "Eco Virtual - Atmosphere." A calm, relaxing song. The room, like a giant mp3 plays out. He waits for his beloved Miyuki.

Still anxious, Andros changes the ceiling TV.

"Weather please."

The ceiling searched for the NHK world.

NHK was premiering its documentary on "History of The Windows 95 3D Maze: American Art."

Andros was watching. Colorful, calming. So... old-school. Something of the past makes Andros feel nostalgic. At home.

Tired. He's not listening to what these Asian-Aryans have to say about our culture. I mean, Andros almost got his "reputation" in "History of Japanese Literature." He dropped out because he couldn't afford it.

That's why he likes going to dark-web cyberpunk websites like Tinshit. Dank Memes. Anarchist commentary that wishes to be liberated from the system. Stuff that you can get in trouble. Oh well, no one is doing a thing about this world. Too utopian to begin with.

Not for Andros. Too lazy to jack himself back in.

If only he was free. Maybe living in a classic house on the prairie. Living with actual animals. Not in this air conditioned, car-hanging-tree smelly, pink fluorescent room. Who cares? When does he ever feel safe?

The noise coming from the ceiling. Something tall stood to the right of him. Looking down.

She had long, brown pigtails. Reaching down against her nipples. She was wearing that classic 1990s maid dress look you see in those cartoons like Sailor Moon. Her arms longer than her legs. Her legs long too. Holding her arms. Obedient.

"Don't give me that 'yes sempai' thing ok?" Andros complained to her.

"Would you like it if I said 'Get the fuck out of bed?'" She retorted back.

"Just kidding," he said, smiling.

She, smiling too.

Rolling over in bed to the right to see her. Looking up like a dog seeing his master back from work.

"You're learning a bit, aren't you?" He said.

"What do you mean 'learning?' Didn't I do everything to please you?"

"What happened to your blue afro? I liked that."

"That was last week. This is this week."

"Haha, I get it, you learned how to think on your own."

Andros got up on his knees and hugged her, trying to wrestle her in bed.

"Stop treating me like a little kid!" She said with irritation.

Falling down on the bed with her. Rolling around together. Now she's on the bottom. His arms on hers. Looking eye to eye.

A smile.

"Um, I had a long day. I feel just like a cuddle," he said.

"Just a cuddle?"

"Yep, just a cuddle."

He laid down. Face to face. His nose on her robot-like cheek.

"Well, how was your day?" she said.

"Not good."

"Why?"

"I don't know, angry."

He didn't move for a bit. She remained silent, like the obedient person she is.

She has a face made of stone. She could take in anything he said. She doesn't have emotions like humans do.

But is she real?

"Miyuki, are you ok?"

Turning her head toward him, "What?"

"Yeah, you."

She was now looking up at the Windows 3D maze.

"Why?"

Silence.

This was the moment Andros was waiting for.

"Um, I know you're a busy person, since you play video games in your spare time, and I care about that... and..."

Conscious struck Andros. In his mind, he was thinking before his spoke his next sentence.

"Does she care? They put her on Soma, I know it. They do it to all these call girls. If she trusts me enough, she would act like a human and be less of the robot. Even to ask her... I love you! No! It doesn't matter. Does she love me? Or is she doomed like this? Does she know the day is coming where she will be recycled? No. I've known you for four years, it's time I asked her."

Andros continued allowed,

"...are you ok?"

Miyuki, with her pale face, looked at him.

"No, what's really wrong?

Andros thought a bit. He said,

"I'm not angry at all. My day, you see, was not that exciting and I don't like going to work. And I am interested to see if, you know, you'e having these same issues where... there is... this kind, of..."

Miyuki said something that caught Andros off guard.

"Andy, I am not on Soma."

"What?" He said.

"I haven't taken Soma in weeks."

A shock. A beat from his heart. Under his chest.

"Wait... really? No way."

"Yes, no Soma. None of it! I'm as human as you can possibly get."

Soma is a drug that keeps call girls in check. Basically, Soma is taken before sessions to make the call girl feel great about the session. If Soma is avoided, which is illegal, then the android itself can slowly transform into a human.

"Why no Soma? You would get in trouble and I care about you and I want you to..."

"It doesn't matter. We all live and we die. Sooner or later, the boss will figure out I'm becoming more human. He will have to recycle me and delete my memories. And I will have a new life and a new partner. I don't die. I think I would actually like to experience death and become a human. I'm going to try and become a human without getting caught. But I'm not so sure. They will find out soon enough. You told me the boss was full of shit too Andy."

"Yeah, I did, and... well..."

It was Andros's fault for exposing Miyuki to the real world. When he was 17, he was new to sex, and that first time he did it with Miyuki was about masturbation. Nothing special. At age 18, he was planning on marrying his high school girlfriend, Jackie Chee. She based her man solely on social status. Dumped. And at the angry age of 19, his viral propounding of "red-pilling" began on Miyuki. Telling how she was a robot, not something like as a human, life is meaningless, and if you really loved anything, you would love Andros. That angsty period of any white middle-American. 21, Andros finished his year reputation online. What is his meaning? Goes in, clocks seven days a week, selling Nintendo cable service to ghetto people?

Andros is a minority in this world. The only pure-bred white person on Terra. He could move to the white ethno-state, but there is something about the Asian beauty that is human civilization on Terra. He's not Asian. But he always had that desire. Especially in Miyuki. Her genes were actually purebred Japanese. The corporations, of course, alter call girls to make some strange, tall anime maid they always tend to look like. Miyuki was becoming more humanized each year and looking less like a stupid anime maid. She was becoming more... human.

Awkward.

"Don't worry about it. Let's watch some TV," she said.

The ceiling recognized that voice. It changed over to MurdarMachene Classics. Old-timey programming.

Miyuki lifted her arms and laid her head on them. Like she was on the beach.

Andros didn't want to seem weak or feminine, so he gave her some room and he moved to the left.

An old show called "World Peace" was on. Controversial for its time, it is now considered a classic, since the young actor at that time, Charles Carroll, is now known as a living legend.

This was the episode where Carroll was acting like a football player. In a pink room, teasing this naive nerdy girl to go out on a date with him. He throws the football violently against the corner of the room. It's amazing. Those same aesthetics of that room Carroll is in, is the same aesthetics that Andros and Miyuki are in.

"I don't get old time humor," Andros said.

"I think they were supposed to act, like ironic, on purpose."

"You mean they don't really mean how they act?"

"I guess so."

He thought about it.

"People from the past are weird."

Looking up. Then looking down. Those cute dinosaur boots Miyuki is wearing. Andros doesn't want to be a perv and take them off. He can gaze at them. Yeah sure. She was made to seduce. Angry. She's more than that!

Wait a second. Andros sees something on her leg. A big blue letter… "S."

He looks back at her. She's enjoying watching Carroll make a fool of himself. ...That smile of hers.

"Um, Miyuki. Is that... a tattoo I see under your... leg?"

She looks back, paying attention. Looks down.

"Why yes it is! How did you know?"

She got up and slid down her dino boots. That big blue tattoo on her leg wrote, "SNK."

"SNK? What's that supposed to mean?"

"You don't know SNK? Well, it was this Japanese corporation back in the day, and they used to make video games. Those old methods where you played with a controller on a television screen? They were big at the end of the 21st century. What happened was, they bought out this other company, called Square Enix, and they were the first to make anime real."

"What, really?"

"Yeah really! There is some heritage to that. I can totally relate to SNK. You know, I think my gene parents, I did some stalking and stuff, and I think my grandfather worked for SNK, so it's cool and..."

"Wait, how do you get out of this place?"

"Shhhs! Don't tell anyone! When you don't see me on Saturdays, I say 'fuck-it' and I dress up like a human and go explore the city."

Andros gawking.

"That is so…"

She's smiling. That long brown hair and those mysterious and sinister looking almond eyes.

"Bad? Haha, I thought you like that. Isn't it cool though?"

Andros thought about it.

"Yeah…" chuckling. "I guess that's cool."

The show was over. Up next, "Aeon Flux." Whatever that is.

"That makes you more human than what I can imagine, I will give you that," Andros said.

He thought about it.

She was in a good mood now.

"What else do you do when I'm not around?" He said.

"What else? Sometimes, I go out to Chinatown… Um, try to walk in the park. You know, I would really like to see a live band sometime."

"Wait, why don't you invite me on your trips?"

"Maybe because I will get in trouble."

"I thought you didn't care about getting caught."

"Yeah, but, like, I need some independence, you know."

"I see," Andros said.

Then those thoughts of his rushed through his mind.

"I can't believe it! A tattoo! Going out on Saturdays when no one is around! Jesus Christ! She's a criminal. If the police find out, I can go to jail too. She is way too... What the hell did I create? Those times when I was upset, I didn't mean to lash out on her. No one cares about me. This is the only person that thinks about me. I love her. I can't say that. I'm going to get caught. Why is she happy now? What's happening? Does she love me now? Oh god. Maybe I should leave and call it a night. I feel good, yeah. I forgot why I came in. Everything is boring and stupid. But... But, tonight is different. I have to ask her... I have to ask if she..."

"Do you like Dolphin Munch?" She said.

Andros looked her.

"Yeah."

The Dolphin Munch came flying over on the floating table. She grabbed the bag. The Dolphins came flying out of the bag and into her mouth they went. Andros bit a dolphin too.

Snack foods in the future are a complicated thing. Dolphin Munch are no different from what you old normies call "potato chips." Dolphin Munch simulate happy animated dolphins, eager to come out of the bag and into the hungry consumer's mouth. Flavors include Pizza, Burger, Chicken, Birthday Cake, everything you can think of. Why dolphins? Dolphins are a nationally known animal. Like say, the bald eagle. If any animal would represent the future they live in... it's dolphins.

Tasty dolphins by the way.

172

Munching away. Ok. What was Andros thinking about?

I guess it's time for him to ask.

"Miyuki. How long will you be doing things like that?"

"Things like what?" Ahe said.

"Things like… that are not call girl like."
"I don't know. I got one life to live, right?"
"Yeah, but… do you have other interests?"
"Other interests?"
"Other interests like… doing something."
"What are you talking about?"
"Like, you know, there's more to life than… doing things."

Miyuki was now looking strangely at Andros.

"What are you talking about?"
"I mean… like."
"Andy, I can do what I want. You don't own me or anything."
"Miyuki, that's not the point! You see, like… I care for you."

Miyuki was now staring at him.

"Do you want to fuck or something?"
"No! I don't. I don't care about that stuff and…"
"You're acting really strangely."

"I care about you and I wish I could do things with you and… you know."

Both turned serious. Andros continued.

"I think of you now as more than a friend. You've been there for me and I always count on you… but I am at that point in my life where I think it's time to do something about our life."

Miyuki, turning red.

"What are you saying? Are you saying I'm not good enough?"

"No, this is about you and this is about what you're doing outside and those things…." said Andros stuttering.

"Like I'm some kind of fucking baby? Who the hell are you?"

"Miyuki! No! I love you!"

Something happened at that moment. Miyuki, angry at him. Something that made her pissed off at her existence. And then those words, "I love you," made her available to listen.

"*Go on,*" she was thinking.

"Please, this is about what I am going through. I had a bad day and I can't stand coming in here every day. I come every week to see you and I know you as this great person and you have so much meaning in my life. I can't leave you and you're someone one different."

Mad, Miyuki looked at him, and said, "Then why the fuck are you here jerking around?"

"I'm not jerking around! Miyuki, I love you. This sounds crazy, but, If I told you this, I would be shunned by my family, I would be hated by everyone, and then there is the consequence of the police," he yelled.

Both were looking at each other. It seemed like the room was silent.

"I love you Miyuki. I want to be with you," he whispered.

Her face, looking at him. As if she'd never heard that before in her life. That these things she was doing on Saturdays, she was alone, looking for attention. She didn't trust Andros enough and thought she could find happiness outside this place. She did call him "Andy," after all. Nothing cuter than that. But now to ask... why?

She looked down. "Why?" She said.

"Because you were there, every part of my life. You gave meaning for me! There is no life without you."

Andros was looking straight into her eyes.

She didn't say anything.

"I love your cute face, those beautiful eyes, your tall body, your funny sense of humor, your charming personality, there is no one like you! I want to be on your side Miyuki. I can't believe I am saying this right now... This is the day... either I go back home or you hate me forever. I'm sorry," he yelled.

Miyuki. She didn't know what to say now. She got up out of bed. She walked the other way.

She looked down. Andros was quiet and upset.

"Do you love me Andy?" She said.

"Yes, I do. I do," he said.

Thoughts were rushing through her head now,

"No way. It can't be. I thought about him too. And... he did like me! This person did like me! I like what I do now. I can't stand being a call girl. This whole life. This pathetic existence. All I ever wanted was to be loved. Not loved for some dumb service. I stopped taking Soma because I trusted Andy. I trusted Andy to be my friend, my true lover! I'm afraid he would say no. Now he's acting like this dumb prince saying that he loves me. How can he? I'm a Japanese android no one wants. Lowest of the low. And he's White. A White person that has expectations in the world! Why would he ever want to approach me and settle with a family! That's illegal. No way. He's not that dangerous... I... No..."

Andros was getting up from bed. Standing right next to her.

"Miyuki. I love you."

"No, you don't," she said.

"Yes, I do," he whispered.

She looked at him,

"Why me? An android? You don't need me... I don't have..."

"Then why did you stop taking Soma?"

"Because I love you!" She finally admitted.

This time, her confession comes out. "I thought you would like me more if I was human. You're right! Being human is much better. Either I ignore the pain and live this miserable life, and pretend everything is ok. It's not ok! Why would you care? You're doing something really stupid for liking me. I like you. And...," she was whimpering.

Getting closer, Andros says, "I love you Miyuki. I love you."

Putting his hand on her shoulder.

Silent. Looking at her, her head looking down.

Whispering, Andros said,

"Let's get married. I will write something for Sunsoft. They'll understand. You'll no longer have to be this thing. You're someone special. We are going to have three kids and, and..."

Andros in his mind, *"I can't believe I'm saying this stuff! All of it is coming out at once! What am I supposed to do?"*

"I love you..."

Miyuki looking up at him... She says, "I love you too."

Her arm on his chest. Looking up at him. She dives for a kiss. Andros, closing his eyes, seeing it come. Shaking. This is unreal. All this is happening at once. This shocker of a kiss. This kiss with her tongue touching his tongue. Unbelievable. Shaking. Both go back. Trembling. She is taller than he is. Strange. What to do?

She runs away into the other room. Andros follows her into the bathroom.

This room, a silver room with holes at the bottom. Looking like a giant silver cube. Lost like in the clouds. She was messing with the knobs.

"Miyuki... I..." trying to explain.

After turning off one knob, she looks at him.

"Take off your clothes. We're taking a shower."

Andros, a loss of words. Happy, to mad, to sad... to, shower time?

She was looking at him. Dead serious. Those sinister eyes. Brown and almond shaped. Unreal.

"Are you... ok?"

She walked up to him and put her arms around his head.

"Andy... I love you too."

Both, lost in the silver cube.

The timer was going off. Once it reached 1, the shower would begin.

Another kiss. This time, it was passionate.

Backed away for a bit.

She started taking her shirt off, exposing her bra... and then taking that off.

Andros's heart beating.

She was naked.

Her dagger like tits. Looking so human. She wasn't an android.

And he had to follow, taking off his own shirt quickly.

She came up to him. Kissing. Deep.

The water fell down from all sides of the room. Like a shower cube.

It felt like an hour, but it was only 2 minutes. The rain smacking against their naked skin.

Looking down on her, while she was down on him.

"Are you ok?" He said, noticing tears rolling down her eyes.

"I like the shower because no one can see me cry."

"I can see you, Miyuki. I love you."

They both embraced for another long kiss.

...Cue in Yukihiro Takahashi's Drip Dry Eyes...

She tucked him in bed while he laid on the couch. He felt like a little kid who was sick and helpless.

"There you go! Don't you move a muscle, ok?"

She smiled while looking him directly in the eyes.

He was shy. He didn't know what to say.

"Sure," the only word that came out of him.

They were the only two in the Rec Room. Everyone else was in the other building for school. Joe had skipped the first class, but it was now the 5th period.

Lisa insisted that he stayed with her.

Bright eyed and animated, she really did care about how Joe felt that day.

She sat right over Joe and looked over him like he was her own son.

The room was the size of a closet. A couch, a TV, microwave, books, a table, all fit snug together like some kind of little Japanese apartment.

"I am always here for you if you feel bad or anything," she kindly said.

Those words repeating over and over again in his mind.

They talked for hours. Four hours now. Their conversations would follow on the lines about personal things to the material.

Joe talked about the music he liked. Like Eurobeat and House music, and the vinyl records he owned.

"I have this one record by Utada..."

"Utada Hikaru? I love her! She has such an amazing voice!"

"Oh, yes she does! I have this one remix by Junior Jack. It is this house version of the song and..."

Things like that. And she would tell him personal stories.

He would say, "My parents are hard to get along with and I wish they were better."

"Yes, I know how you feel. I don't talk to my dad either. It's really hard for me. It's different when you have someone who is verbally abusive. I can totally understand."

A situation like this would cause anyone to become close together.

Naive and young, Joe would get too personal with himself.

"I wish somebody would notice me in school or at least what I do. I don't understand why anyone wants to make fun or bully me."

"Really? You're the type that would be the popular kid in school."

"No, I am not. No one understands me. In fact, I never kissed a girl in my life."

"Never kissed a girl? Wait, you never kissed a girl before?"

"Yes. Not once."

Lisa looked dumb founded. She was some kind of Chinese-American geek that thought of herself as an animated real life anime character.

She wasn't a student of the school. She actually worked and volunteered for it. She was 23, Joe 19.

She continued, "Do you want to get your first kiss?"

"What?"

"Your first kiss. I can kiss and you don't have to think about it anymore.

She smiled, looking at him. Her glaring white teeth were shining.

Joe thought about it. He acted so natural to what she said. His processing speed didn't pick up the exact words that she'd exactly said. So, he said back, very awkwardly,

"Sure."

Lisa hunched over to Joe, slowly, closing her eyes and kissed him on the left cheek.

In his bed, Joe did not know what was going on.

He looked at her. She looked back at him.

"And you need your second kiss!"

She leaped forward and kissed him again on his cheek.

183

"And as well a third kiss for good luck!"

And she smooched her face into Joe's like some kind of embarrassing kiss from an aunt. Holding down her lips and making the classic "Ma-wa!" noise letting go.

Joe smiled and looked at her. She smiled back.

"Now, you don't have to worry about it anymore!"

That last one kiss was pretty close to Joe's mouth. And her tongue licking on his skin. All too real.

That was almost a make-out session.

Joe did not know what to say other than to chuckle and say "Thank you!"

"you can trust me to do anything Joe!"

And it was like that. Incredibly comfortable and caring.

Then they would talk for three more hours! Having Hot Pockets together, watching silly stuff on YouTube, and her sitting on his legs (close to his soft erection) while talking about everything that was meaningful about life.

Six and half hours later, when the bus was coming to pick everyone up, Joe had to leave.
This would have never happened if Joe did not skip his first class. And now, she made him skip every single class today.

"I have to go Lisa, it was so much fun hanging out with you today!"

"Let's do it again another time!"

She said it like a little kid out of some high-school anime.

"Give me a hug!" She said.

And she hugged Joe like a snake. Deliberately trying to squeeze him to death. She was making mumbling noises. It was about a good 30 seconds too.

He had to leave and get on his bus home.

"Ok, bye Lisa!"

"Bye Joe!"

This time, she went up to him and kissed him on the lips.

"Have a good day today!"

"Ok," he said, waving to her as he got on the bus.

***

"You see," he said while sobbing, "I don't even know my own self! I was abused when I was a little kid. I didn't have any childhood friends! I barely made it out of high school. Then what about all the colleges I dropped out of! Where am I going?"

"You're so lucky to earn a double major in English and Communication. Most young adults your age never earn such an accomplishment. How do you feel about that?" The psychologist said in his Austrian accent.

"I mean," (sniffle) "What's the point now? I'm not like anybody else. I'm different. I'm struggling with that. What I am supposed to do? I don't anymore. I feel, I feel, bad about myself. I'm a loser!"

The psychologist turned angry.

"Hush up! You are making matters worse. You need confidence in your life and you have to improve your social existence!"

Crying, the boy said, "I told you, I hate going out to the bar! I hate meeting new people. They are all the same! Evil and wicked!"

"This is not about them! This is about you! You need to find a place in your life!"

The psychologist was quickly examining his papers. Checking notes.

"Starting tomorrow, you will be in group therapy session with another patient like yourself. Both of you will realize that the world is not as bad as you think it is."

The boy was still crying. He didn't know what to say.

"I guarantee you this will work! You are paying for the best service there is."

This is a proposal. A proposal for our *own* state.

California is only miles away from that county every White American loves.

Japan.

Therefore, California would be the center of Japanese culture in America.

Unfortunately, here out on the East Coast, especially New York, it's full of Chinese.

The Chinese, and then the Japanese.

The Koreans, The Filipinos, The Thai, Vietnamese, Mongolians, Indonesians, Singaporeans...

Did I forget some groups? I don't mean to be exclusive.

Are you a cute Asian? With a nice baby-boy face? Slick hair, obedient, funny, submissive, all about family?

Great! You would belong in a... *Asian-Aryan* state!

Wait, what? "Asian-Aryan?" What do you mean by that?

Believe it or not, California is really an Asian-Aryan state. Though I've never been over there, (my grandma has), I would like to visit sometime.

I am quite comfortable over here on the East Coast. But someday, all Asian-Aryans will have to make a pilgrimage to their homeland. Japan? China? Those are surrogate. I'm talking about an American experience. Asian-Aryans live in a diaspora right now.

188

"Ok, hold up. What is this all about?"

Well, are you White, or are you Asian? Both? Awesome.
Either / or will do.

White Male, Asian Female couples are crucial to the Asian-
Aryan state. Yes, we are also accepting Asian Male, White
Females too. But let's get to the gritty truth. Stats show
"WMAF" is much more abundant in this age of
"multiculturalism" and "Diversity."

Yes, there is a lot of "Asian culture" in San Francisco.
More like Chinese. Daly City is a town for Filipinos too.
Good candidates. Silicon Valley? Elite WMAF's live there.
Let's start with the small things and then move to the big
things!

The "majority Asian cities" are a recent phenomena. Asians
will turn things Asians. That's cool. But we're talking *about*
Asian-Aryanism!

*A culture is an extension of race. It shapes the people that
live their lives.*

A foreign culture, but nostalgic to home. I'm not talking
about "anti-white," white genocide. No. I'm pro-white,
believe it or not. I call myself white too! And I don't want
to see Asian genocide either. No "anti-Asian" policy either.

The tug-of-war is real. Whites pull at one end, and the
Asians pull at the other. I guess that's what you get when
the two cultures mingle. "Pick a side!" They say.

Hear in Philadelphia, the WMAF gap is real. They both
enjoy their company. Both parties will flirt with the White,
then flirt back to the Asian. These WMAF's, going to work

every day and then having fun on the weekends. They know it's real. They don't have the words or means to describe what's going on.

Ahem... Asian-Aryanism! It's real!

"That's racist and sexist! How could you think of such a thing?"

...We're not interested in your type. Go be a cuck somewhere else. Set on your autistic, universal blinders! See if your Chinese wife cares!

(For newbies, please go on YouTube and check out Greg Johnson's speech on "The Refutation of Libertarianism." A Big red-pill for ya).

Not a cuck anymore? Good. Keep reading.

She likes you. The first time you ever dated an Asian girl. The first time you had sex with her. That time she sucked your dick. You know who I'm talking about. When you first started dating and you realized there were more options than "white' girls.

Sorry ladies. This is a White-male-to-White-male talk right now.

You're not a cuck. Wait. I just called you a cuck. Not *that* kind of cuck. The cuck that dates an Asian girl and says it has "nothing to do with it."

The problem is... *it does!*

I'm speaking for you believe it or not. You're not a cuck in the sense that you truly do love your Asian girlfriend. I

190

know you had those thoughts about marrying her too. And then in your late 20s, you realized you should "settle down," and marry white because there was no one else important.

Wrong choice brother.

You should marry your Asian girlfriend.

You belong to Asian-Aryanism.

White girls... do you understand where I am coming from?

Any handsome, intelligent, strong Asian men you ever met? We have those problems, I get that. It's a part of existence. Not something to be ashamed about. You haven't met the right ones. I know the right white girls know what I am talking about. That smart guy that brings you into a whole new world that's not about living in a boring, Nebraska suburb anymore. Asian culture, it's so genuine! Girls, you know what I am talking about.

As for Asian girls, no need to explain. White men rule! I'm not a cuck when I say this. White culture is so unique and special. Innovative, creative, social, orderly, apologetic...

I love being a part of White culture. And I love Asian culture too.

If only there was a way to synergize the two...

You guessed it, Asian-Aryanism!

No need to be offended! Everyone deserves a place on their own. White countries for white people. Asian countries for Asian people. I'm really talking about this American situation right now. You see, we don't live in a "multicultural" and "diverse" society we imagine to be in. The system has created more racial groups.

And when Whites get to choose other non-whites to be their loves... guess what? Most whites choose Asian. Sorry blacks and other non-whites. White men like their Asian women.

"Sorry, no offense, but it's true!" Milo Yiannopoulos says on his radio show.

Multicultural society has failed us. It rather created the soon-to-be Asian-Aryan people.

Whites boys, Asian girls, you know it's true. Why does this world not benefit us as a "people?"

It's time for that calling.

So back to that Asian-Aryan state of ours... where will it be?

We can't live in an upper-class bubble. I understand Chinese love social-status and can be gold-diggers. No. We don't need that. Go to Silicon Valley. We are talking about the working-class Asian-Aryans.

An Asian girl for every White boy! That is one thing we will offer in this society. No more degenerate sex and dating competition. Every single girl is some kind of Asian-Aryan. Magnificent!

The "women question" is out of the way. Ladies, be yourself.

First language is English, second language, Chinese/
Japanese/Korean/others.

English is the priority! But we love our broken languages,
don't we? (Donald Trump impression)

The dream of the future! Anime is real! The hope is real!
We will be these futuristic, beautiful pan-White/Asian
people!

No white genocide, no Asian genocide. We need our
patents. Without them, there would be no Asian-Aryan
people. We respect our ancestors!

We love our own new Asian-Aryan traditions. Most
WMAF practice these traditions without knowing these
things. Dinners in the city, electronic avant-garde music,
going to concerts, expensive art galleries, eccentric family
outings… do I need to explain myself?

All those Asian-Aryans that went to go see Shin Godzilla
that night in the movie theater… More WMAF's than
anything. Beautiful. If only they knew about this… this
state… Where is it?

What would this place look like?

Manhattan, Philly, Tokyo, Chinatown? A mix of everything.
Don't think too much about the architect.

It's not like an anime fantasy land or vaporwave, cyberpunk
Akira city. No.

Average. Safe. Fun.

Like that cute Chinese girl with the thick black glasses and hair. Loves her white boyfriend.

The Asian-Aryan state is not intimidating! Not militant! We are like a free-love society, except only Whites and Asians are allowed.

A city exclusively for Whites and Asians. For now, we will keep it a secret, and call a city-suburb somewhere in California.

I get it.

Someday, we are rising. We are in bars, at show venues, Asian restaurants, art galleries, your local suburban community. Right down your city block holding hands together.

We are everywhere. Keeping this relationship a secret.

…No longer. Goodbye cuck behavior!

Hello Asian-Aryanism!

All WMAFs welcome!

Welcome to…

…I don't have a name. Not to be arrogant.

Well, well do you guys live?

Most major, metropolitan liberal cities? Ok.

Walnut Creek?

…I can trust you…that you are on a mission… for Asian-Aryanism.

>;)

...I know what you're thinking. This "Asian-Aryan" thing sounds "degenerate," "cuck-like," or "Jewish," and that the promotion of racial mixing is what the alt-right is against!

First, I do not advocate racial-mixing. I advocate "Asian-Aryanism."

If the alt-right is to succeed, then everyone, and I mean every homogeneous race on this planet, needs to have some sense of self-determination and racial awareness for a greater good. That sounds great, doesn't it?

Therefore, Asian-Aryanism acts like an alt-right scene for Asian-Americans. An anti-sexist, anti-nihilistic, anti-hedonist, Men-Going-Their-Own-Way determined to achieve an Asian wife, a professional job, and three Hapa children.

This is for every Asian living in America, for every Asian-loving White person, and... for every half White/Asian child who...

Stop right there!

"Hapas?" ...Hafus?

"No, no, no, no! You said you were against racial mixing! They don't have a proper racial background! These bastard mutts and their sinful parents! How selfish of you! Either they choose their White side or their Asian side!"

Umm... Ok... but don't they still have "degenerate" genes even if they chose a side? They are neither pure White or Asian. So why push it under the rug?

I think the best solution... for your own European Imperium or imagined ethnostates, is to simply put all those dirty "race traitors" into multiple cities each the size of Wilmington. Call it an independent state.

Please, whatever you do, don't go on a "day of the rope" scenario and kill all the pretty Asian wives of the already handsome and athletic young white men who are married to them.

Yes, you heard right, White males / Asian female... and Asian males / White female married couples with Hapa children, are allowed in the Asian-Aryan country. They must show the utmost devotion to a pan-Western-bastard-Confucius/Shinto culture of racial devotion to the new great race. That simple. Let it be known that to live as an Asian-Aryan, one must become an "Asian-Aryan."

What's that?

First, those people you call "weebs" are just misguided White Americans that need a healthy diet and daily exercise in their life. We want our men to have bodies like Adonis. And for the women? They are already beautiful and caring to begin with. You may call our women "fish-like," "insects," or "gook-faced," but you just don't understand.

"Asian-Aryanism" is a prideful term, not a degenerate one.

"Enough science-fiction! Why are you even advocating such a stupid and troll-like philosophy? Can't we all do normie things and not think about such postmodern problems?"

I have been getting tons of hate mail from the far-right, the far-left, normies, and disgruntled Hapas. I don't need to argue with Asian women that are married to White men. All they have to do is self-realize what they have done.

You know, the far-right will say I'm "Jewish" and will want to throw me in the oven. And then the far-left will say I am "insensitive" and not treating people as universal.

Guys, use your mind for once. This is not about you.

Asian-Aryanism is so controversial, that both far ends of the Western political spectrum hate what I have to say. I believe, however, that both political sides know that Asian-Aryanism is righteous and true.

"What the hell is Aryanism? You sound like a Nazi! Better yet, that's an oxymoron. Aryans are NOT Asian!"

Ok, "Asian-Aryanism" is a whimsical term. And it has certainly got your attention. But in the context of "Aryanism," what "perfect" race are we talking about?

Once again, I don't have to advocate racial mixing.

…Because it is already happening in most major, liberal metropolitan cities in America!

What is that perfect "Asian-Aryan" race I am talking about?

White boyfriends take their Asian girlfriends to punk rock shows, art galleries, nerd conventions, and vegan restaurants.

Have you seen that before?

And later in life, the children of those WMAF's are sent to Chinatown or mainline elementary schools. Always in a hip, urban, suburban, stuff-white-people-like, approved location. Namely, Trader Joe's and Starbucks are incubating the new race of people.

And just remember this... they can't be "white" now! I would call them Asian-Aryan!

However, do point this truth out to any normie with an Asian girlfriend or wife. We like to call them a "new-cuck." You get something like this:

"Oh no! This has nothing to do with me discriminating and choosing an Asian wife! I love her! And that was a spiritual and universal choice! I would have chosen anyone! But I choose her! Race doesn't matter to me! Why do you care what she is?"

Yeah right.

White man, you made your choice.

"New-cucks" are real. They are worse than just a "cuck." Not only do they race-mix, but they deny their future destiny and race. Sadly, pretending everything is universal. And then they go ahead and practice Asian culture and say it has nothing to do with that. This is exactly new-cuck behavior.

A race mixing White man or woman who refuses to put their racial consciousness first, is an opponent of mine.

I am actually a European advocate. I want to preserve both the European and Asian races. Without them, without Mom

199

and Dad supporting us, we would not have this beautiful culture called Asian-Aryanism.

I am not anti-white, and I hate Noel Ignatiev. I do not want to abolish the White race. I know "Jennifer Suzuki," the pen name of some erotic-writing troll, would like to see Asian-Aryanism coined as the new White people. Maybe that will happen if the new-cucks win this war. But I would like to see in the future separate and conserved people. However, Asian-Aryanism is happening and is not dying down.

We are Angry Hapas, Asian-Americans, isolated White nerds and WMAF/AMWF couples, who just don't give a fuck anymore and want to yellow-pill the Western world.

You heard right, I would like to yellow-pill you.

Trust me, Asian-Aryanism is a friend of all forms of nationalism and a friend of all far-left, edgy street culture. We are avant-garde and normative at the same time.

If you have an Asian girlfriend or boyfriend, take pride in that. Chances are, you might well have kids someday! But make sure they are on the White side of things.

Am I confusing you now?

Look, make sure they argue and defend a state which puts both their own White/Asian interest first! We live in a society that denies White racial consciousness to White people and to every single half-White person.

Now are Asian-Aryans the new White or Asian people? No. You could "whitewash" Asians, and then they become "white." And for the opposite case, you could send a Hapa to go study in Northeast Asia so that they become more "Asian." But whatever happens in the future, your Hapa children will develop a symbiotic destiny with other like-minded Asian-Aryans. "Whitewashed" or "Asianized," the crossroads are leading to one destination.

Trust me, this has so much to do with White culture as it has to do with Asian culture. It's why these dual personalities will eventually become a part of a single "Aryan" identity.

Sorry, I am not advocating for other non-whites, like Blacks and Mexicans, to racially mix into Asian-Aryanism. Asian-Aryanism is a unique religion exclusively for the relationship between White and Asian people. I really don't care about "muh freedomz." God bless whatever you do. But Black Male / Asian Female coupling isn't a thing. And don't try and call it "Afro-Asian-Aryanism," because what I am doing isn't a joke either. We are against the multicultural and diverse paradigm.

If you would like to associate with a darker and black race of Asian-American people, then make up your own institutions and find your own idols. Start with Billy Blanks and Jero. Look up Ganguro and Gyaru fashion (I love that stuff). Become self-determined!

I will support you and be an ally, but I will defend my Asian-Aryan people first. Don't race-mix because you want a utopian, universal, brown-skin, "cafe-ole" society. I will then become your enemy.

I am against what Richard von Coudenhove-Kalergi once said about an "Asian-Negroid race," oddly being formed to make a civilized Ancient Egyptian one. Nope. I don't like that one bit. I get where he is coming from, but he is wrong on several points.

Kalegri knew there was going to be an Asian-Aryan race. I know that feel bro. However, he was such a hypocrite to support universal race-mixing in the underclasses, and the preservation of a single racial (((elite))) class at the top. I am not Black, and I have none of those racial traditions and background. I don't want my future children and grandchildren to look like Whoopi Goldberg or Aubrey Drake Graham. I want them to look like aesthetically pleasing, healthy, Asian-Aryan anime characters. To say Whites and Asians should mix with African genes is quite offensive and destructive to what both Western and Eastern societies have built.

No, I am not advocating what Kalegri has said before. He is totally misguided and was confused on his own racial identity. I am rather criticizing and fixing his utopia. He himself was, by birth, an "Asian-Aryan." And he could have been one! However, he has failed to see his potential as an Asian-Aryan and then forced a multicultural and Jewish elite, one-world government ideology instead.

The multicultural paradigm ironically has created a large influx numbers of WMAF coupling and offspring than ever before. In the diversity market, White men will choose Asian women over everyone else. The truth is harsh. This is another reason why the single-race utopia will not work. White men don't want other non-white women, unless they follow their code of attraction. That is the tradition of Western Civilization. Asian women automatically win in this discourse. The ideology of Multiculturalism will be around so as long as White men truly get what they want from the globalized world, and that is the "model minority" of Asian women and their culture.

202

Watch R.A. The Rugged Man debate Jared Taylor on the Gavin McInnes shows. Who are the two major races that are creating racism? "Asians and Whites," The Rugged Man says. Those are the two new racists. Together as one.

When that ideology of "diversity" and multiculturalism is truly gone, Asian-Aryanism will replace it. Imagine all these new-cucks, with their Asian wives and half children, praising themselves in the future rainbow nation...

"We now live in a multicultural society! Everyone is racially mixed and we are free of racism!"

...Not!

Those fools! Whites and Asians are the only ones that have mixed, and now they are a new race of people that is ultimately perfected! That old paradigm was just a bridge for the East and West to perfect one another in a chaotic world!

Again, I am against multiculturalism and diversity.

Asian-Aryanism is a "Plan B" philosophy if White Nationalism loses against white genocide.

The word "Aryan" is certainly whimsical. I am not referring to a group of "Asian Neo-Nazi" roleplay and cosplaying found on some image board. What I am talking about is real. You might think "Asian-Aryan" is an inappropriate term, since why call normal people Nazis? I am talking about a group of radical people that exist today and need to yellow-pill the Western world in order to self-actualize new-cucks into Asian-Aryans.

Why is Asian-Aryanism happening? Well, again, who wants to date a fat White, Amy Schumer-looking, blue-haired feminist? That of course, is a unique byproduct of the culture and nature of White women. And I will promise you, you will not find that in Asian girls (they have something called "yellow feminism" by the way, and that's just a love for White men).

Asian-Aryanism is mainly a group of guys on the left-wing faction of the alt-right with Asian girlfriends. Some of us are ex-MGTOW who realized that not all women are bad, and only Asian women are the redeemable angels.

This is who I am. I am an Asian-Aryan. As well with every other yellow-pilled WMAF/AMWF couples and Hapas. We grew out of this "weeb" phase and now we are adults approaching reality.

We all make choices and stick by them.

We have all have duties, responsibilities, and growing up to do.

I will continue to spread the Asian-Aryan ideology over on my YouTube channel and beyond. Feel free to criticize what I am doing.

The future will one day belong to everyone who wants self-determination and racial awareness. And that also belongs to every racially mixed group of people.

Asian-Aryanism has so much potential.

Now, do you have an Asian girlfriend/boyfriend or ever wanted one? Do you like Asian culture and the West? I think you should join the movement!

Mike's so-called "best friend" comes up from Texas once a year for like five seconds. And that's right now.

There is literally nothing to do in Paoli, Indiana. Smack in the middle of nowhere.

But this is where Grace found her Craigslist boyfriend. Online, and located here.

Yeah, she could have stayed in New Jersey. She was going to Indiana University for the hell of it. Her Chinese family has the money for it. What's there to lose?

She's really Americanized. Hardly knows any Chinese. Flat chested. Ugly looking little urchin thing she is. Hardly washes her black hairs. Sounds like a guy. Problems written all over her.

She was raped at her pizza delivery job back in Jersey.

Not if I believe it either. I don't even know how it went down. "Rape" these days means many things. Looking at her, you can tell something is up.

But in Edgewater, New Jersey, she had everything. Handsome, tall, blonde white boyfriends that all have some interest in sports. She could have any of them at her will.

Pick any one. They would have loved to escort her on a date. She had all that when she was 18.

And now, to throw it away and change completely at the age of 22? Does she even know her own self?

Mike and his boring friend John sitting outside the front porch. Drinking and talking about nothing. Grace had a thing for knitting. She promised one boyfriend, long time ago, a Cthulhu doll. She never did make it. She claims she has amnesia.

And she laughs all the time about every possible comment.

"Hey, you guys have the NES Classic? You know, it has like all those classic games on it," said John.

Mike rocking his chair,

"Oh yeah! We got it! I got it a few weeks ago! I got it for $60! Not gonna lie. It's in the room hooked up!"

Grace laughing.

"Hell yeah dude!" John said, raising his shitty APA.

"Like, I'm so happy I got this thing. I can relive my childhood experience and play Zelda again. I love Zelda so much. Best video-game of all time!" Mike said.

Mike is 35. Yep, and to "game" dirty Asian pussy at 22, not sure.

Grace wanted to move out of her house. She did it before with a boyfriend in Ohio. That guy left her while she moved in. And then she had to live alone in Cleveland while her surrogate text boyfriend was Frank.

Frank, that's his name. Frank. The boy she knew since elementary school. When they would play Four corners as little kids, she would act like a funny jester and pretend not to play.

She is still like that today.

Mike, that fat slob, Pitt-Ohio, truck-loading bumfuck. Ask him the benefits of "multiculturalism and diversity." He might say something like, "I am so glad to have an Asian girlfriend. Otherwise, I might not even meet her in this part of my life!" Something low-IQ and backwoods thinking like that.

Mike loved Legend of Zelda.

How many of these types in the millennial generation think like this?

Link. A blonde caricature made up by the Japanese. Everything these lonely, anti-modernist, inexperienced, mute teenagers want to be. Not a good thing. Especially when at work, Mike will imagine himself as Link. Not willing to be a man about things. This 30-something-year old that hasn't read anything by Jack Donovan in his lifetime.

He doesn't know how read. Or pick up social cues.

He took 9 years to graduate from Indiana. That includes debt, dropping out, working-part time, and all that time... could have been spent on a Master's or even becoming a PhD student.

Time is valuable. And he thinks he will live forever. Give him another beer and more anime to watch. A feeling that won't last long.

Until tomorrow comes.

A byproduct of Mid-west depression? Most likely. Bad genes? Yeah, that too.

Grace was texting someone on her phone as she watched Mike and John babbling on.

Frank? Yes, it was.

You see, they met again when Frank bumped into her at The General's Store. A board game store in Jersey.

Frank was 20 at the time. No experience at the time. Still none. Grace was supportive of Frank. And still is.

Then there was that one time, on Frank's 22nd birthday, when Grace kissed him goodbye as she got on the train. Does she like him? She still calls him "Frankie," as if he was still in elementary. Like if Frank is still 8 years old.

That was three years ago.

All the things that Frank will do to get Grace's attention. They have hung out many times before.

Frank, a young, intelligent, physically fit, quirky, cute looking White male.

He knows about Mike. Never met him, doesn't want to. Why him?

A 25-year-old with potential in life. Then compare him with this washed-up, 35-year-old guardian. Eww.

They say older men have a higher chance of seducing younger women. Hugh Hefner, that rat.

As men get older, their power increases. As women get older, they become weak and pathetic. You can see the vice-versa to this formula.

Grace and Frank's texting went something like this:

Grace: Relationships are never black and white. That sounds like a difficult dilemma. Because on one hand, you probably want her to be happy, right? But on the other hand, it seems like you really like her. Also, graduating is hella stressful.

Frank would tell stories to get Grace's attention. They were not real. He had to put up this facade to make Grace feel he was something. When in reality, Frank is alone. He doesn't have proper friends to go see every week. He never drinks, does drugs, or anything of that stuff.

Not once has he ever had sex.

Frank: Did your bf graduate from IU?

Grace: Yeah, in 2014. Took him 9 years though. I think it will take me 9.5. So, all good :).

Frank: 9 years???? No way. Borrow money and hire tutors. You can climb the ladder.

Grace: Haha no, it will take me that long because I need to have 5 years of lessons. I am on semester 2. The other classes I could finish in 2 years if I felt like it.

Frank: I hope we can hang out soon. I shouldn't text too much. I know it's Sat night and the cliche is everyone does something. Not tonight for me, I'm alone.

Grace: It's okay! I am only doing something today (usually I'm not) because Mike's best friend only comes up from Texas once a year for like five seconds and that's right now. Once the semester is over, we can hang out. I literally only go to school and work right now :(.

Frank is still going after this little ugly girl. Why? That's at least what Grace is thinking. He's so strong and beautiful looking. Compare him with Grace, out of her league.

Love is the only thing that connects them together.

That hard feeling… Frank has been in this relationship with her for over 5 years now. He has been rejected three times. Will he make a fourth attempt? "Four corners," that's a good joke.

Grace has to put her phone down for Mike's attention.

"Yo, Gracie! Can you show John where the NES is?"

"Yes! Ok."

She goes off like an eager cartoon character.

Does she even know she why she is with this older guy? She once tried to associate herself with being a lesbian. That didn't go too far. And what about her family? They have probably disowned her. The dad and mom could care less about who she marries. A half-White/Chinese child produces a Chinese according to them. That's the big Chinese plan. Produce children for the benefit of China's society. Foolish white people.

Ugly she is. Ugly he is. Whatever.

Frank is still a slave to her love though. What is he going to do when January begins? He is going to graduate with a degree in English. Possibly by next year, attend a graduate program in creative writing. That works.

What about Frank? What does he do?

He was seeing someone else too.

He didn't tell Grace... pretends this is only a proxy for the relationship. He will be back to Grace's commands. Eventually...

Driving in his car, Franks plays music through his Android phone. His CD player in the car is broken. Sometimes, he will only turn on the car radio for WPRB Princeton. Interesting stuff. Most of the time, stupid indie rock stuff. Frank would rather waste his monthly data on YouTube songs. It works.

Driving while it's cold outside. Bitter. Driving to the weekly game night. Different store, different town. New girl. How things change in three years.

Frank was ok with the situation. Really not. The trauma about Grace is there. Everyday it's there. If only something new could happen and then the past can close like a book. Having constant anxiety about life, having tons of disappointments and failures, what is the meaning of it anyway? To worry is more meaningful than to be happy. It's like this every morning and before bed. Grace. What happened to you?

KMFDM is a great band to listen to while on this cold, mid-west highway. Joy Electric too if the mood is about being happy. Frank was not the macho type nor did he want to be something he was not. Grace was made for him. The reason why she is not with him was her own choice. Sadly, Frank was hardly with her. He wanted to be with her. She was too busy with her own life. Frank came from an upper to middle class background. Grace was all upper class, but was envious about the lower classes. Her family kicked her out, for obviously Chinese reasons. Frank was so lucky to be with her. Grace could care less. Before he knew it, she was on someone else. What was something Frank did not have? Grace was looking for social status, fun, meaning, and independence. Frank had all that. But it just didn't match Grace's expectations. They were in wo different worlds. Frank tries so much. Tears, sweat, blood, everything. He'd been there with her since elementary school. And no, sadly, she didn't want him. Maybe it's for Frank's own good. Maybe Grace will always have the upper hand. It just didn't work. Grace wanted to live out her own perverted life, even if it meant disobeying her family. Spoiled she is. Not Frank, nope.

This new girl Frank is seeing is somewhat spoiled.

Her name is Tracy. Another Chinese girl. Unlike Grace, who is 4 years younger than Frank, Tracy is 7 years older than him. She's also got a Masters in Psychology too. Frank has nothing but the job he's got. Two different cultures. There's always that one culture that has nothing and are like white niggers. And then there is a class above this, with some money, but spend it wrong, and they could end up like them. And where Grace comes from, tons of money, but her failure to compete, and her family excommunicates her, and she is down at the bottom with a secret paycheck sent by her family every month because they love her. Tracy belonged to the highest class. Mom, Dad, her two sisters, all got PHDs. Being the youngest, she can easily obtain this last PHD in psychology and then take over her father's business in Kokomo. But you know how Asians work. Mimic and copy the material, forget about it, and keep their position. Nothing has happened but their age. Can you tell a 30-year-old Asian from a teenager? They never age even when they grow old. And then all those repressed memories and experiences that haunt them.

Tracy had a thing with Frank. One time, they were cuddling and Tracy whispered in Frank's ear, "I'm going to stab and kill you." All cute like some little kid. She had a thing for violence. S&M shit. Even though Frank was her second boyfriend. Her first white boyfriend. Never did she have sex. Once Frank pulled down his pants in front of her. All she did was punch and bite it. She enjoyed it a lot. Such a suppressed creature.

Frank had to see her every Tuesday night for board game night. Frank liked board games in his teen years. Now, as he gets older, that's passing by. The painful memories of Grace haunt him. Board games remind him too much of Grace. Did she even like board games? She lied one time and told him "Video games give me anxiety and that's why I don't play them." Oh yeah. Then that one time Frank, his best friend and older brother were in the vintage video game store, and without noticing anything, Grace saw him with her then boyfriend. Run out of the store. That bitch. She didn't last enough with him. And now she is with this 30-year-old fat fuck she met on Craigslist. Trust Frank, she is a mentally disturbed person. To have abuse like that only makes Frank crawl back for more.

Six years of his life, crawling back to her, texting her, meeting her at discrete locations, seeing how life is. Frank always wanting to live life with Grace until the day he died. Most people do this anyway. But he can't with her because of her own reasons. It's so easy for her to pretend that she's into him. Yeah. She lies. Sometimes, she will block Frank's text simply because she doesn't want to answer him. Even more radically, she makes a broken promise, "Let's hang out." Never will she! She skipped Frank's 21st birthday for no good reason. Frank cried that day and told his parents. One of the worst days of his life. On his 22nd birthday, however, she felt so bad, they fucked in his college dorm. That's how radical the relationship is. She looks like an ugly little fish monster. Frank who is taller than her is ok with that. Deep down inside, Frank knew he was a masochist, a sadist. That's why he always went back to Asian girls. Not only to remind him of Grace, but to fulfill his desires that he is a loser. A painfully feminine, orbital beta male, that waited for things to come towards him. He wasn't a normie. He existed in an environment that was not for him. He would be better off being a character in a Wes Anderson film. He deserves to live his life in New York City surrounded by beautiful people and the eccentric upper class. Nope. That's not going to happen. A pipe-dream. That was what Frank suffered through. Just like all other white people on this planet.

As Frank walked in the store like he always did, seeing all the stupid happy white nerds, doomed to their nihilistic existence playing Magic The Gathering, he was there to fulfill his desire with Tracy. The pain he'd had to go through was greater than anyone else. He knew, not out of arrogance, but noble righteousness, that he deserved his

Tracy. Frank had zero confidence because of his verbally abusive and bipolar father. Over time, he had learned to overcome such feelings. Frank was beautiful. Tall, slim, always shaved, was on the cross-country team. But he was always a queer, an anti-normie, someone working the system without any friends. The worst thing you could do in the American system! Work in this life is only to make money, only then to buy hedonist things with it. This is what is called "freedom" in America. The freedom that Gracie has is the equivalent freedom Frank may get whatever he spends it on. Sad that the system is like this. That's why Frank was a secret white nationalist. Angry at his own people. If only white people were more like Asians and then they were submissive to authority. If only white people purged their decadence and all became Christian. Maybe. That might be happening with the alt-right. However, Frank loves Asian girls. That's not going to stop him.

Every second of his waking life, he thinks of that Asian girl that could've been his at the age of 19. What did he do wrong? How could he repent. Could he have saved their life at that age? Was he too stupid to begin with? What is wrong?

Nothing. Nothing is wrong. Last Christmas, Gracie texted Frank "A Merry Christmas!" He obviously started it. And this year, Ronnie Martin and En Esch wished him a merry Christmas through email. His favorite musicians of all time! Everything was going well. And he wished Gracie again with "merry xmas." No reply. What a bitch.

Sitting right next to Tracy, life is different. He could focus authentically on board games and admire and enjoy the company of Tracy. Fulfilling the gaping hole that was missing when he was an inexperienced teenager. He did something right. Still... even though she is better than Gracie... she still could be better. She could be a whole lot nicer and called her "Frankie."

That could be a start. Nope. Something happens dating Chinese girls over and over again. Their personality comes out in different traits.

And he remembers the day when he was 21, in Kokomo hanging out with his older brother and his girlfriend. His older brother's girlfriend was scary enough. Frank bought the 4th pack of Android:Netrunner cards and his favorite album was Dancehouse Children's *Songs and Stories*. And then he started to contact Grace again through Facebook. She was in the hospital. Hospital for what? Suicide? Things started to take a turn. That was 4 years ago. That's when she was using him again and things were getting more serious. This was hurting his own psyche. He met Grace by accident at a goddamn board game store too. By accident when he was 19. Stop it. Just stop it. The pain is too much for Frank. The day he went to the first Netrunner regional was the day after he was haunting out at Grace's million-dollar family mansion. So much was going on in 2013. Memories flash and Frank sees them.

What could've been.

He was too nervous to drive and head to rely on his friend to drive him places. Still, he took a bus to go see this one An Asian girl to have sex with. It was worth it. Any way to get away from the reality, the story, that was not unfolding his way. He was the loser in this story.

All this was going on in Frank's head while Tracy bothered him to play a board game.

That first time, when he started to like Tracy. They were playing Cosmic Encounter and he lost against everyone. That January of 2015. That same night, Grace promises to come over and play games. At the same time, she tells him she cheated on Frank. Crying non-stop. He never forgave Grace for 10 months, until that Christmas. How damaging this relationship is. Why doesn't he just quit?

The sad truth is, Frank can't. He is with Tracy and will be with Tracy until they get married and have kids. It will go that far. Far enough to bring her to white nationalist events too.

...Times Square, Manhattan. Fiddler's Roof Restaurant. This was the end of a long day meeting with White Nationalist types. All together, a room of 80, dining on Irish chicken and cheap pasta.

This was Jack's fifth time at a meeting like this. He's pretty used to everything now. He just graduated college with a degree in English. Every year, even before his Freshman year, Jack was invited to these private nationalist events. He loved it every time he went. As he grew, he matured, and so did his philosophy.

But tonight, he was in a state of confusion.

A real life shitposter, a skinhead who'd criticized Jack's online work, teased him a bit.

A giant Asian girl outside with her giant lips and her closed eyes. One of these blade runner, dystopian advertisements that were all too real.

"Hey Jack! She's saying, 'I will suck you long time!'"

Laughs around the table. Jack had a thing for Asian girls. He went as far as to defend them on discussion boards. Jack wanted to be a white nationalist and have his cake too.

He just ignored the jokes and took it as compliments.

Jack was thinking about something.

"When did you graduate Seth?"

"Oh, it was about in 2009. At that same time, however, I was writing for Radical-Epoch too!"

"And your book never came out?"

"Well, I don't know if I really want to release a book of all my silly articles. Especially about the one with GAME and the midget. Not only that, but even speaking in front of people. What the hell am I going to say?"

"You know, if I was going to speak tonight, I would speak about my undergrad life, and everything I experienced."

There was some silence. Jack had a think about this for a bit.

"I mean... Like... Being in college today is different than it was, say, even a decade ago! Have you experienced the feminist or social justice warrior types on your campus?"

"Fuck no! Everyone was bored as shit. There were frat parties but that was mainly it."

"Well, I went through them. Everything. I went to four different institutions in my life time. First, there was community college, and then state school in the city, back to a frat boy school on the mainline, and then finally ending my last two semesters at a private college-on-the-hill. All girls' school to make it even worse!"

Jack continued.

"The thing is, if you want to know why I like Asian girls... is that I was caught up in that whole scene. There are no pretty white girls to date. All of them are whores or just blue-haired feminists!"

Suddenly, Dr. Ryan Smith came over to sit by Jack. Smith was the organizer of these Radical-Epoch events. Jack looked up to Smith like he was his real dad (his real dad by the way was verbally abusive to Jack; he really doesn't exist at all in his life). Smith sat down and looked straight into Jack's eyes. Jack was trying to continue his speech, but had to recap or at least get Dr. Smith into the speech.

Jack said, while looking both at Smith and Seth.

"Look, at my school, all my white male friends were role-models to me. And all of them had pretty Asian girls! Asian girlfriends! I didn't know what to do! To be accepted within the video game or anime club, I had to date an Asian girl too. So you know, I had to get one! It wasn't my fault that they were there!"

Dr. Smith was looking directly at Jack.

"Ryan! What do you think about that? I can't get out of that situation! It was going to happen that there was no pretty white girls there to rescue me! How are we supposed to save these white guys and get them onto white nationalism? Are they doomed too? It can't be just a mistake or bad behavior! I couldn't escape the scene, you know? How is a young millennial supposed to get out of a situation like that?"

Ryan's face was serious, thinking about it, a little disgruntled. Deep in thought. He didn't have anything to say back.

Seth butted in,

"One thing for sure, is my kids are going to be red-pilled before they have a chance to think about college. Probably, they will not go because college is now a scam! Just don't buy into their bullshit. You know. It's survival at that point."

Another kid by the name of Mike butted in,

"Once they get a fucking job, and they start learning how to pay for their own living, then they can't bitch and complain about social justice or live in a dream world. All of them are using mommy and daddy's money and spending it to be decadent fucks. They are not learning anything at all. It's teaching young people to be dependent on others in life and basically teaching them how to be good liberals!"

As Jack was trying to listen in on Mike's comments, Dr. Smith walked up and moved to the other side of the room. He probably thought everything was good. ...Jack wished he could have got a good answer from an experienced professor. Especially a radical one.

Seth said, "Once you learn about the bigger things in life, like how neuronic the Jews are and why people are brainwashed, then maybe you will come to understand that people are weak and are led by strong men."

Jack replied, "It's not that simple. Think about the French revolution and how European people wanted to be free from monarchy. That is a white people thing too. I don't think the Jews are responsible for every evil on this planet. This is a rational reason why people like, you know, Asian women. Especially, during this confused time where all this stuff has happened within 60 years and we as a generation have created a harmonious... vibe... with one another. I don't have the answers, but I have a feeling."

"Yeah, whatever."

As Seth closed the conversation, dessert was served. Chocolate cake. Time again to eat and keep things quiet.

The cake was good. No complaints. But Jack was deep in thought. Tonight was so much fun. If only he had an Asian girlfriend and show all his friends how happy he is. He brought one Asian girl to the last two conferences. She even sucked his dick once. But soon after they broke up. He is single at the moment.

Jack could hear Dr. Smith's words in his head again from earlier on.

"You are a young adult, and you are going to grad school soon. I know you don't have an Asian girlfriend. You have so much potential in your future!"

Those were some inspiring words. All of that was true. ...But if only Jack had an Asian girlfriend.

The struggle to be single at such a young age. If he had a choice, he would get married now and have three kids.

Eat healthy, exercise often, look good, have a great paying job, dress nicely, promise security, be on time, and have a nice personality. That's what everyone wants. And hopefully, the supernatural will of an Asian woman will come to Jack if he practices those things. He has to be open about his desires too.

It was so much fun tonight. Unreal. So much fun being at these white nationalist conferences...

Still, where is he going in life?

Personal recommendation from BOLD & DETERMINED to find a suitable wife:

Picking a woman from your own country and culture is always the best solution. Unfortunately, there is wholesale, systematic destruction of marriage and family in many first world countries, especially America and England, which has narrowed the options tremendously. One may have a broader selection if he were to go abroad to another country where marriage and family are still valued. But, and this is a big but, think long and hard before you marry a woman of another race and father half-breed children.

Remember, it is best to marry a woman of your culture and race. If that option is unappealing for the reasons described above there is a whole, big, wide world for you to choose from."

-Victor Pride, How to Pick the Right Wife.

(https://boldanddetermined.com/pick-the-right-wife)

"To be real identity politics, however, it has to be based on a real identity. We are not just creatures of our own time and place, since we reject the false and meaningless identities that the current system offers us: deracinated individuals, citizens of the universe, children of nowhere, defining ourselves by the plastic products and postures we consume and discard. Instead, our identity is defined by our whole biological and cultural lineage, which leads to the present day and cannot be re-routed to some other time and place.

We reject the modern "identity" because it is false, because it does not fit us, because it makes us miserable and base. But modern individualism can only be fake if we already have a real identity, although we might be largely unconscious of who we really are. Therefore, the answer to the modern malaise is to discover who we are and live accordingly, to be authentic rather than fake. It is no answer to simply replace the predominant fake identity with something equally fake but merely more eccentric or marginal. Adopting off-the-rack systems of ideas or living in the past are symptoms of rootlessness rather than solutions for it."

-Dr. Greg Johnson, The Relevance of the Old Right.

...How does a white nationalist, or even the single white man, overcome his desire for Asian women?

Should this be forgotten about? Should this even be thought about? Isn't this just a normal reaction for any type of women? Why is the focus on Asian women?

I don't think this is a fetish either. There are many legitimate reasons to love them.

Besides, if you really overcame the desire for "yellow fever," you're just a normie like everyone else.

...You're a racist for even considering marrying your own race!

And I thought it was progressive to marry outside the race!

This is exactly how complicated the issue between White men and Asian women go.

I could be fair and also talk about the relationship between Asian men and white women. However, it is almost non-existent. This is exactly like Black male and white female, a mistake by the women's side! The non-white always gets the benefit from this transaction.

To be honest, men have the influence in any relationship! That's why there should be a focus on WMAF. I do believe there can be equal footing in any relationship. The Asian-male / White-female complex is exactly like the WMAF relationship. Once WMAF establishes, AMWF soon follows.

The problem for white nationalists, however, is that race-mixing is a burden for their cause. The multicultural paradigm promises exotic and beautiful women to any successful white man. Choice is good, but in the capitalist market, it is a consumer choice. Non-white women are exclusively "market choices" white men can make. It gives them the impression that they have a sense of liberty and freedom. In reality, people prefer to be with people like themselves.

When given the opportunity to race mix, few people actually do it. Race mixing tends to happen with unfortunate people of lower-classes or environmental causes. Jewish people have been known to race-mix only for the cause of social status. Still, they preserve their race and treat other half-Jews abiding people to their cause. It's the same with the Chinese, who use people who are half-Chinese, or "Asianization" to benefit the cause. They benefit by associating themselves as "Chinese" but are not fully Chinese. This advances the cause of China's pillage and rape domination, a classic scenario that has been practiced by the most ancient people.

Some have argued that is the multicultural paradigm that we live under today. White populations are being swamped out with other non-whites so that European people can be extinct through constant race-mixing. This is the motivation for white nationalism. Nationalism must secure the existence and future for white children, culture, and society. Nationalism is at its peak in the current year and faces its biggest opponent: globalism.

It was only half a decade ago, that America was a 95% white European country. Slowly, through open borders and suicide rates among whites, by 2017, white people are now only 50% of the country's population. If current trends continue, white people in America will be extinct, or at least be a 10% elite class in a North American racially-mixed Brazil. The reason why open borders have happened in the last few years was because of several things.

There was the civil rights movements, Jewish activism in the far-left, avant-garde literature that became professionally accepted by corrupted academics, the rise of technology, the internet, and "postmodernism." The baby boomer generation of white people became resistant against their parents, and sought to create a more free and open-minded liberal world. As we as a generation have personally have experienced, we as a people never really benefited from this "diversity" and our depression soon followed.

But we have to ask ourselves, "Why in the world did we think non-whites would benefit in a white society?" This, of course, has been around since the days of colonialism. And "post-colonialism" is merely a politically-correct version of it. European people have been fascinated with other races around the world. As of this century, white people have concluded that they are the master race! And that namely, Western civilization is a byproduct of white people! The people who invented philosophy, law, justice, and innovation! And all these things were sought after by other non-whites. Karl Jaspers argued that other non-whites had innovation through "the axis period." Well, that was just wishful, post-Nazi thinking. White people have realized they are the only supreme people in a world where no one understands them, creating an innate loneliness. As Rudyard Kipling would say… white people, since the end of the Victorian era, have been under "The White Man's Burden." That is, "should other non-whites of the world be proselytized into the great culture called The West? Or, should they be left alone, preserving their self-determination with the aid of other white people, benefiting and handicapping their societies to be like us?" That question still haunts us today.

Race-mixing has been an answer to improve bounds among whites and non-whites. This, as soon as it was realized after the influence of the 1960's, has created mentally unstable, and almost retarded, mixed-race offspring. Like a bastard mutt found in the streets, race-mixing has its consequences. Ultimately, the way our PC culture has tolerated this happening, is by giving ultimate handicaps, infinite victim status, and inauthentic sympathy to mixed-race people. This is the way our media pushes them on a pedestal. From Adrian Tomine, a punk zine comic writer to now New Yorker cover artist, to Macintosh Plus, a supposedly mixed race people who popular the hipster music genre of vaporwave. All with support from white liberal elites that feel they need to suppress the truth and play dumb to the realities of race.

This is the situation what White nationalists are up against. On the other hand, there is the Antifa, who also believe they are fighting against "racism" and "fascism." They have a similar philosophy to white nationalists, but are playing a game of living their adventurous, robin-hood like lives. Nothing is to be accomplished through the practice of lifestylism. Lifestylism is a byproduct of our system. The system wants us to have strange and contrasting lifestyles, so we can keep consuming and be non-threatening to the establishment. This is why I am very concerned about street activism and the petty fight between left-wing protesters and right-wing protesters. I would rather want to create a dialogue between the two parties and achieve goals. Personally, I do not advocate being a part of a "protest culture."

We have to ask ourselves why we even got in the mess we have today. Jared Taylor once said that white people have a strange and innate, pathological altruism that goes against our best interest. Hence, why all our white women today are bitchy and shrewd feminists that fail to find their potential in life. This, with low white birth rates, creates dysfunction in our society. And then, in New York City, we have flashy lights and exotic businesses on every corner. Money to spend and things to buy. As if we as white people set in stone this futuristic and hedonist society for us to enjoy. We put aside our religion, our faith to family and folk, and we would rather be considered atomized, egalitarian, individuals or special snowflakes. We know these things have caused problems in our society, but they have been improved by us.

We could say those "nasty Jews" are the eternal enemy against us, and against our will, created everything we have today.

I am not falling for the scapegoat cause.

It is an eternal conflict within us as white people.

We like certain things, yet we have scorn for them.

Why are we sarcastic, ironic, and consume all the time? WE don't even care for basic needs, like the pursuit of happiness. We refuse to grow up, and by the time we are adults, we are still hapless teenagers with a suit and tie and social problems. This, I don't think, is natural. I don't take pride in any of the things I just mentioned.

The Millennials are a generation that has decayed traditions created by Gen-x and their parents, the originators, the baby boomers. Why should we continue with them?

In today's society, we are so confused, that we can't trust one another, institutions brainwash us only to get a buck from us, and everyone is constantly in the cubicle work-farm or home alone, running away from everything. WE have lost trust.

Postmodernism snidely celebrates this confusion and calls it "progressive."

This is damaging. It is why I am against postmodernism.

We can all agree that we are in a coming age of "red-pilling" and racial awareness. White millennials have two choices. Either continue the lie and live a bourgeois life, or be honest with reality, and then live a bourgeois life.

If we have more people that realize that we are living a lie, then those in positions of power can shift the paradigm leading towards white nationalism.

And this will lead back to what I am really trying to tie this all in with. What I call... Asian-Aryanism.

This is where everything is heading towards!

One big Asian-Aryan society, and every other unworthy non-white suffers from both liberal egalitarian delusions and "gibsmedat" disorder. That is where our future is if we don't address this issue.

The "new-cucks" I have mentioned are radical non-believers of truth. They are bourgeois just like everyone else in this rotting, existential system.

If we know Asian-Aryanism is inedible and will happen among non-believers of white nationalism, how should we reduce their influence while keeping them at bay?

I have three proposed victories for white nationalism to overcome Asian-Aryanism...

First, there is something called the "disenchanted victory." That is, young white men, who first date Asian women, or at least try to be their friends, will realize how non-white they are and then gravitate towards their own women. This may include pointing out that Asians might be fish or insect-like, that they are a culture of imitating and shaming, and that they are primitive to us. This is the most common method of getting white men out of Asian vaginas. However, this also has a consequence.

This technique is no different than the cliche joke about the gay guy in the military. It is the cliche "Keep it in the closet" and "Don't ask, don't tell" policy. Rather, what happens is that men become repressed about having desires for Asian women, and then they become arrogant towards others. This is an inauthentic method of going about being a white nationalist. It is not really a proper argument and rather prudish behavior. Ryan Andrew's book *The Birth of Prudence* touches upon this matter. Supposedly, the main protagonist will magically dump his hot Asian girlfriend in favor of Western Civilization and all problems are solved! Unfortunately, this is prudish behavior. I know many white nationalist friends who give me this story. One friend even told me that his first girlfriends were Asian, but now he prefers White only. He said that dating Asian women were like riding with tricycles. And now he tells me that white women are the grand Imperium! Foolish, I would have to say. If given the choice, men would rather prefer tricycles forever than a better challenge. Just like how 1% of the world's population is fed by McDonalds alone. This prudish behavior, or even psychotic ubermensch self-improvement, does not address the issues of Asian-Aryanism. It ignores it and calls the ideology a "phase," just like having teenage angst. However, it remains the most common method of getting people over towards white nationalism, but will say that people who held the "disenchant" emotionally unstable and are looking for meaning.

The second method victory against Asian-Aryanism would be "weeb nationalism." This is the idea that nerdy white boys and girls would unite only under the identity of a fake Japanese one. Because we live in society where white racial consciousness is denied, white nerds will often pretend they are something they are not. It's not okay to have an explicit white identity, but it is okay to have any other non-white identity. The most popular non-white identity among nerds is an Asian one. Mainly being Japanese. This is ironic because the masculine white men we often try to woo over, look after black culture for masculine values. White and nerdy boys and girls will show up to any cosplay or video game convention looking for other autistics and delusional whites to find comfort, pretending they are something they are not. Most white nerds who pretend they are Japanese or Asian are called "weebs." Often, these weebs will show up aspects of Stuff-White-People-Like culture without even knowing it. It will soon turn out that white weebs will date each other, given the chance when they meet. This is the crypto promotion of white nationalism. They still believe they are an anime character to an anime no one is watching, which is still reproducing within the white race.

The weeb nationalist method is the most common tactic to persuade weebs to stay in their race than go on the Asian-Aryan side. Although, the problem with weeb nationalism is that it will eventually lead to Asian-Aryanism, that is, if their desires are not controlled enough. This will lead back to the very first method, the disenchanted victory, if a weeb ever realizes that Asian women are different.

The third position I recommend, and which I personally advocate for, is "trauma therapy." Often, whites will have desires for Asian women after an intimate, close or sexual event with them. If a White person lives in Ohio, and meets his Asian girlfriend in New York City, and then right after, goes back home, he is going to feel issues of abandonment, since he is tied back to his own community which is all white. This abandonment issue will lead to some form of depression, and eventually back to the disenchanted victory.

Abandonment is like being in prison. Eventually, the lonely whites desire for Asian women will bubble up and will lease out when he has an opportunity to escape his boring doldrum. So, isolating a white doesn't help either.

Trauma therapy, which is the most hardest of the methods to obtain, is to gather a group of soon to be Asian-Aryans (or proud Asian-Aryans) and discuss why they love Asian women together as men. This method is extremely beneficial. If taken with good turn, they could help out white nationalism. If not, then this will give a better opportunity to become Asian-Aryans.

Too many people are being "red-pilled" and growing up out of the SJW and liberal facade culture that dominates our sleep. They will be only encouraged to make anime real... if it is not real.

I believe a common goal among white nationalists is to find dialogue with other races and mixed-race people, so they can understand that people prefer to be separate. Asian-Aryans can be great allies for white nationalism. If given the right opportunity, Asian-Aryanism can be a proxy ideology for white nationalism. Again, to use the method of "the tricycles on a bike." However, Asian-Aryanism will revolt if not checked, as they are looking for an authentic life to live out too.

People are different. Whites might even have half Asian/white offspring before it's too late to realize the purpose of white nationalism. What are they to do with their children?

Convert all the children under Asian-Aryanism and everything will be fine! This is where white nationalism can be beneficial.

We simply cannot put all non-whites into an oven. This is extremely unfair and disgusting. Beautiful Eurasian women should be princesses for Asian-Aryans.

Nationalism is about crafting the whole world into separate places where a person can be oneself ...Exactly like the state of Israel. With progressive technology, the incoming masses of useless people, and at the same time, the liberation of information, people have become more ethnocentrically aware. Ethnostates are becoming a real, cultural phenomena. If is to happen, Asian-Aryanism will have its own state too.

About the Author:

Pilleater was a college student and is now a hip, unemployed podcaster and internet troll. His influences include Tim Biskup, Seonna Hong, Scott Wills, Rob Renzetti, Alex Kirwan, Jim Woodring, Kurt Halsey, Rodney Alan Greenblat, Mineo Maya, Adrian Tomine, and everyone else in the lowbrow art scene. In his early days, he was an agent for Realicide Youth Records. He lives as an apathetic loner outside of Philadelphia.

...Thank you, Robert Stark for getting me out there.

Also, I want to thank Alex, Haarlem, Pozwald Spengler, Rabbit, James Nulick, and John for support.

www.asianaryanism.com
www.youtube.com/pilleater
www.twitter.com/realpilleater
www.mineomayafanclub.blogspot.com
www.starktruthradio.com